SKULDUGGERY

Printed in Australia
First Printing: February 2023
Shawline Publishing Group Pty Ltd
www.shawlinepublishing.com.au

Paperback ISBN 978-1-9224-4466-0
eBook ISBN 978-1-9224-4467-7

A catalogue record for this work is available from the National Library of Australia

SKULDUGGERY

PAUL RUSHWORTH-BROWN

This book is for my children Rachael, Christopher and Hayley and my wife Clare Brown whose support and patience made it possible.

CHAPTER 1
MISSING SPARKS

Times were difficult in 1603 and there were shenanigans and skullduggery committed by locals and outsiders alike. Good Queen Bess has died, and King James sits on the throne of England and Scotland. His reign is not without controversy as on the eve of his second Parliament, a Catholic plot against him is discovered. This was to become known as the *Gunpowder Plot.*

England erupted with sectarian violence and the promised religious tolerance of King James was finished. The country was in turmoil as the relationship between James and his Parliament deteriorated. The country faced financial pressures and increasing inflation.

Among the poorer lot, times were changing. Food was scarce, there was widespread poverty and Catholics were tortured and imprisoned for their beliefs. A Bill was introduced to Parliament which outlawed all English followers of the Catholic Church.

Two hundred miles away on the moors of Yorkshire, a family's lives would be forever changed by these events.

The bleak Pennine moors, a beautiful, harsh place close to the sky, rugged and rough, no boundaries except the horizon which in some places goes on forever. Green pastures and wayward hills, the colours of ochre, brown and pink in the spring. Green squares divide the land on one side of the lane and on the other. Sheep with thick wool and dark snout dot the hills and dales. One room cruck cottages scattered, smoke billow out of some and not others. Dry stone walls divide and fall, a patchwork of green, green and greener. Long grasses whisper while swaying in the chilled wind, waiting for the summer months. As the sun goes down, the silvery beck glistens amongst the ghost-like trees that line the bank. The countryside sings its songs to the beat of the day, a chorus of echoes from the undulating hills. Clouds line the horizon and widen the gap between the blue and the moor.

Thomas Rushworth, a man of medium height, and a face weathered by the punishing wind and harsh burning summer sun of the Pennines, the boyish good looks hardened by winter months, invigored and alert. Thick dark brown eyebrows crowned honest, deep-set eyes, a straight nose and chiseled chin.

A broad-brimmed straw hat, sweat-stained and tipped slightly, shadowing his relaxed expression. The hat peaked a weathered, leathery countenance and allowed the thickness of the bowl like cut to be seen reaching the nape and covering the top part of the ears. The hat, slightly too big but held down with a worn, sandy coloured broken string at the base of the crown. A shaven shadow, but with a slight nick on his long chin from the old steel straight blade that he used. Long white shirt greyed by frequent washing opened at the top to show bristled chest hair, speckled with grey, peeking through the top. It hid his brawny upper arms, born of hours upon hours in the fields, tapering to the wrist and his rough, calloused hands. A pinkish-red tattered sheepskin tunic frayed at the bottom stretched and secured across his chest with two sheepskin ties. A brown jerkin dyed with madder plant dye and mutton sleeves wide at the top. Tight, dirty, cream coloured hose covered both slender legs from hip to waist, stained from the day's cultivations. The 'codpiece patch', a similar colour to the hose, covered the groin area but Thomas did not find the need to advertise his masculinity unlike some others in the village. Dirtied leather and wool shoes tied at the top gathered loosely around the ankles, and the thick sheepskin soles tried their best to keep out the unfriendly earthen chill. He was not a tall man, but one of confidence, which made him seem taller. His bearing was upright, although he walked with care, before putting weight down on the foot lest a stone pierce the thin leather sole.

It had been a severe winter, and a ten-week deep freeze had made life intolerable for Thomas and his family. Trees split, birds were frozen to death and travelers told stories of the Thames freezing, stopping river traffic and allowing people to walk across it. Thomas remembered the stories his father told him as a boy about the great drought that had brought king and country to its knees and the memories of the summer of the flooding which spoiled crops and decimated food reserves. Thomas was only a youngster then, but he could still remember the feeling of the pangs of hunger that he had felt when his mother had carefully split what little bread and pottage that they had into small portions for their family of six. 'Better the pangs of hunger than resorting to eating the unimaginable that others in the village had succumbed to,' his father said. He sat there on the hard-uncompromising wooden stool warmed by the central fire, smoking his clay barrel-shaped pipe and silently staring into the flames.

The shine of the fire reflected off his face and dried the film of mud that caked his leather and sheepskin foot coverings. The aroma of his manly smells from the day's labour, made more pungent by the heat of the fire, drifted up his nostrils but was quickly overpowered by the recent release of steamy faeces by the cow that lived in the corner of the one room cottage.

He could feel the breeze sneaking through the gaps in the closed shutters, and it reminded him of the daub and wattle repair needed to the exterior of the far wall. A job for the summer after seeding had been done, he thought. He watched a spark fly out of the fire and briefly ignite a piece of straw, forcing the English mastiff to reposition itself to a safer distance from the fire. The flame was quickly extinguished by the dampness of the trodden straw and the wet earthen floor, which at times flooded with the spring rains. All the while Bo, a frisky rat terrier situated himself at one corner of the hearth, one eye on his master and one on the hay crib, his favourite hunting spot where he could be assured of a scratch and pat, a reward for the erasure of a pest.

His wife silently stirred the pottage in the cauldron, ensuring added grain didn't stick to the bottom. The gutted rabbit snared last night added a wealthy protein to the mix, a treasured prize.

The smoke from the fire mixed with the sweet aroma of Thomas' pipe tobacco, which filled the room that was perpetually smoky. They didn't have a chimney and it was far too early in the season to open the shutters at night. He wondered one day if he would have a chimney.

Bo, hearing a familiar rustle in the hay, pricked up his ears and focused his full attention on the mound of hay currently consoling the cow and one lamb. He lifted himself slightly from the floor, shifting his weight forward he moved slowly yet purposefully toward the sound, but not giving too much away so as not to frighten his quarry.

'Pssst, what is it dog?' he said, with a broad Yorkshire accent.

Bo briefly looked at his master before instinctive focus got the better of him, he wagged his tail in anticipation, lifted his head and bolted towards the slowly moving hump of hay with no thought of the unexpectant lamb who darted clear of the charge to take refuge on the furthest side of the cow who, used to such commotion and unaffected, continued to chew on its cud.

The English mastiff, a huge dog which lacked the agility of his tiny friend, wagged his tail. He watched Bo run and dive snout first into the mound of hay, lunging at the rat. It was almost half his size and almost as long with the tail; seizing it by the mid-spine he flung it out of its cover, being careful not to get bitten in the first instance by its razor-sharp yellowed teeth. The rat, sensing its demise, landed awkwardly but recovered to flee along the bottom of the wall. Bo bounced out of the hay and pounced again, but this time biting harder through the spine, cracking the vertebrae, and demobilising his prize as it flew to land with a thud. The English mastiff barked a sign of support and watched on as Bo tended to his prize.

'REX BEHAVE,' yelled Thomas.

Rex excitedly wagged his tail, but laid on all fours with his head held high in anticipation. Standing over the wet, limp, bloodstained carcass, Bo watched for signs of life. A sudden twitch sent him into a frenzy. Taking the limp carcass by the neck, he savagely thrashed his head from side to side. He lost his grip at the last moment and watched as the rat slammed against the wall. Rex barked again. Bo pounced once more, not biting but sniffing and nudging with his snout to prompt signs of life. He gave his victim one last deep bite on the neck, released and bit again. Satisfied he had completed the task, he stood over the rat and lifted his head for approval.

His master grabbed its long tail and flung it out the door for the village dogs to consume. Bo tried to follow, but Thomas closed the door quickly in anticipation, then scratched him behind the ears as he returned to his stool beside the fire. Rex took up his position at Thomas' feet, waiting for a pat of acknowledgement for his part in the hunt.

The mastiff raised his broad skulled head painted with the black mask that was common to the breed. The dog could hear footsteps, but they were recognisable, so he wagged his tail and put his massive head back down on his robust fawn coloured paw. The latch lifted and dropped and lifted again. The door opened, sending the smoke from the fire curling and scattering toward the rafters as if to flee the sudden chill in the room. Thomas turned, raising his hand in an impatient gesticulation. 'PUT THE WOOD IN THE HOLE LAD!' he yelled angrily.

Wee Tom came running in, quickly followed by his older sister Margaret, who closed the door quickly so as not to acquire the ire of her father.

'Where have ya' been lad?'

'Running on the green.' Young Tom paused in front of the hearth and looked to find the mastiff, who lifted his head. He let out a slight giggle and ran to where the dog quietly laid. Young Tom sat on the dog's back and grabbed his ears. The dog lowered his head and patiently grumbled, allowing the young one to have his way. Tom bounced up and down on the dog's back while a slobbery line of dribble fell from the corner of the dog's shiny lip and pooled on the dirt floor below him.

'Leave the poor beast, Tom!' shouted his father.

Margaret walked over and lifted Tom balancing him on her hip. 'Come on brother it's almost suppertime.'

It wouldn't be long before she had one of her own God willing. But who would want ta bring up a child in this world? thought her father. His other daughter had already participated in the naming ceremony and now lived away. He rarely saw her because Haworth wasn't the most accessible place to get to, especially in winter, but he thought of her often and prayed for her happiness each night.

Agnes spooned some of the three-day-old pottage, to which she had added grain, peas, beans, and onions from the garden. A piece of dark rye bread was placed on top of the bowl and handed over to the master of the house.

'Ta wife, I could eat the lord's horse all ta myself,' he said with a mischievous smile.

'Husband, I don't think Lord Birkhead would be happy about his missing horse,' she replied without a pause, smiling cheekily.

'Well, if he gets any fatter, the horse will be crushed by his girth, so better the beast be used for a grander purpose.' All who heard laughed at the imagined sight of the horse falling foul to the weight of the lord of the manor. All except Grandma Margery, who sat with her back to the far wall, away from the chill emanating from the door. She was fighting hard to keep her eyes open, the relaxation of the muscles in her neck allowing her chin to drop and be jolted back into contraction less she misses the evening meal.

She noticed the rest of the household laughing and leant forward 'What did you say son? I didn't hear,' she said with growing impatience and a curious look.

The poor dear's hearing is all but gone, thought Agnes. *She couldn't have that much longer left, but she is a wily old wench that one and she sees and hears more than she makes out.*

'It's alright Margery, Thomas were just enlightening us on the health of the lord o' the manor.'

The old woman, never backwards in letting her thoughts be known, 'Lord o' the manor? That bastard worked thy father to ta grave he did! 'Without as much as ta muchly for 20 years of service, he couldn't even pay his respect at his funeral. He knew he had the king's evil, and he still worked him from dawn to dusk while he wasted away. No royal touch ceremony for him.' Her face wrinkled in a scowl.

The excitement had taken its toll, and she began to cough, a chesty rasping cough causing her breathing to labour. She finally cleared her throat and spat the phlegm into the fire. It landed on the hearth rock and started to bubble; the circumference of the red-green blot dried as she sat back to gain back her energy expended during her rant.

She wiped the remaining spittle from her chin with her sleeve and watched as Thomas broke bread and dipped it into the bowl, quickly stuffing it into his mouth to ensure no drips were wasted. He retorted and opened his mouth as the steam emanated and his face went red and contorted from the hotness of his first bite. Thomas quickly waved his hand in front of his mouth, fanning, trying hard to cool the hot morsel of soaked bread which burned the roof of his mouth. He could already feel the loose skin forming and he knew it would be a day before he could jostle the loose dead skin from its place with his tongue.

'God wife are you trying to kill me? It's hot enough ta start the blacksmith's forge.' He declared while taking the clay tankard of ale from Margaret who, smiling, had reacted quickly to her father's dilemma.

He guzzled the ale, soothing the roof of his mouth, but the area still stung when he touched it with his tongue.

'Maybe you won't be in such a hurry ta scoff down thy dinner in the future, son,' Margery whispered.

Unperturbed, Agnes stirred the pot and replied, 'Well 'usband what did you expect? It came from a hot place. Would you rather it cold?'

She poured some of the stew into another bowl for wee Tom, blowing on it to cool its intensity.

Tom ran over to climb up on his father's lap. His father quickly placed his bowl on the stump beside his stool, grabbed him around the waist lifting him to blow raspberries against the skin on his stomach, much to his pleasure. He giggled, so his father did it again before sitting him down on his lap, roughing up his hair tenderly. Agnes handed her husband the wooden spoon and the bowl.

Agnes looked on contentedly, smiled and then frowned, remembering his sickness as a baby, and she thanked the Lord for his mercy.

Agnes served young Margaret, who took the bowl to Mother Margery, who had temporarily dozed off. Her hair covering wimple was lying crooked on her forehead as she leaned her head back against the wall. Her eyes were closed, mouth open as she breathed a deep, chesty breath. A deep, guttural vibration emerged from her throat. Her thick woolen kirtle bunched at her feet, holding a collection of straw attachments.

Young Margaret touched her on the shoulder. 'Grandma, you awake? Here's thy tea 'n ale.'

'Of course, I'm awake daft lass, did you think I was dead?' As she tried to nod the grogginess away. 'Not yet. Soon, but not yet.' Grandma straightened her wimple, sat up straighter, well as straight as the curve of her back would allow, took the bowl and began to blow on it, coughing again as she did.

She took her first spoonful. 'Delicious Agnes, even better than yesterday and the day before that,' she proclaimed while lifting the wooden spoon to her lips to blow on it before placing it in her mouth.

With an utterance that only Agnes and Margaret could hear, she mumbled, 'Might need to stoke the fire a bit prior to serving. Hot pottage keeps the chill away.' Looking down at the bowl cheekily to erase suspicion from her son.

Thomas looked over to see Margaret and Agnes smirking at Grandma, trying hard to keep a stiff upper lip. He couldn't hear what she said, but he knew that he was the bane of her muffled colloquy.

'DON'T GIVE US ANY CHEEK MOTHER OR ELSE I'LL HAVE YA' SENT TO THE DUCKIN' STOOL!' Thomas roared in a threatening tone but then became quiet and complacent seeing the humoured sparkle in the eyes of his wife and daughter.

Margery looked at him, grunted a sound of inconsequence and took another spoonful, winking at young Margaret.

'Dead, she'll probably outlive us all,' mumbled Thomas, noticing Agnes' contempt for his lack of respect, judgment and lack of empathy.

Thomas watched his mother through the smokiness of the fire. The lines on her forehead told many a story like the rings of a tree. The Reformation, the Black Death, The War to which she still remarked being always loyal to the House of Lancaster. Her praise for good Queen Bess.

He heard the bell of compline ringing, a reminder of prayers and the coming of night, and it reminded him of the coming day's work.

Wee Tommy still sat on his father's lap; his father helped him guide his spoon into his mouth, albeit more liquid dribbling down his chin than making its target.

'Gew on son, get ta ya' mother.' He set him down and gave him a pat on his behind, watching him proudly as he walked over to her.

Grandma had finished her pottage and sat there leaning forward, wooden bowl and spoon still in her lap and a tankard of ale still half full dripping its contents because of the angle that she held it.

CHAPTER 2

THE OLD WOMAN'S SECRETS

While Agnes fed the wee one, Thomas sadly reminisced. He looked over at his mother, remembering the difficulty she had faced in his father's last days. Weeding the hide through the day, cooking, washing, and tending to father through the night. She was much younger then, but firm and of high morals and wished no ill of her husband. As a young lad, he often wondered if they loved each other because they never showed any affection outwardly. The question was answered many years later when his father got the sickness; he could hear his mother quietly weeping in the darkness of the night and his father trying to console her between raptures of coughing and wheezing.

By day he continued to work the fields, often kneeling in the dirt trying to fight against an uncontrollable fit of coughing. You could hear him trudging home through the mud, a constant drizzle making it difficult for him to see. His cold, wet clothes clamped against his feverish skin. Eyes deep in their sockets darkened by rings of tiredness, foreboding and worry, for he knew not what would become of his family once he was gone. He would stagger in out of the weather and collapse on the bed, often spouting delirious ravings as mother undressed him and dried him as best as she could.

Often, he wouldn't get up again and remained there to battle the growing ache in his chest, coughing to try to get some respite from his clogged airways.

His persistent choking cough was always followed by the splatter of blood in the rag that mother, Margery, continually rinsed and gave back to him. The wakening, delirious ravings and night sweats, the chills, chest pains and shortness of breath and the irreversible weight loss. His mother tried to feed him broth, but most times it would end up coughed over mother and dribbling down his chest. This all ended one night when the coughing stopped, and the wheezing quietened, eventuating in dark, solemn, peaceful silence.

Not much had changed for Tommy, now all grown and called Thomas, son of Thomas, after his da. He thought back to the times as a youngster. His father and mother had to tend to the fields for the lord from sunrise until sunset, pruning, weeding, scaring birds in spring, harvesting and ploughing in summer and smoking and weaving in autumn. They had to spread manure to prepare the fields for the crops, prune branches, harvest the hay, and cut the wheat. Not to mention collecting the brew from the lord's favourite cottage to appease his alcoholic tendencies and wash down the pheasant and imported wine.

They were good times and bad, happy times and sad. Around harvest time, father would often carry him on his shoulders through the fields on a Sunday after church. He would swing him around by the hands so that his feet acted as a sickle to cut down the wheat. They would play hide and seek in the long wheat stalks. He was always able to sneak up on him, but he knew his father allowed him to, laughing and acting surprised when he did.

He never spoke much of his family, saying that they moved up here from Mould Greave when he was a very young lad. He said that his father left for war one day and didn't return, even though his mother waited and waited. One day she got the sickness and passed, leaving him and his elder brother and sister to fend for themselves.

Thomas was only seventeen when his father passed, but he could still remember looking through the gap between the black loose-fitting curtain and the wattle wall, put up to separate the living from the dead. His last sight was one of sadness, as his mother Margery and her cousin silently dunked cloths in cold water and gently wiped the soil of a lifetime from his body. Margery was solemn but did not cry as she realised the living hell that had tortured her husband for the previous three months and now she knew he was at peace.

He laid there outstretched on a makeshift bench put together with some locally sourced planks. He was completely naked except for a loincloth which covered his more modest parts. The once muscular physique had wasted away and the bones of his ribs protruded through the pale, loose skin. The muscle in his arms had deteriorated, and now unapologetically sagged loosely to the table. His unshaven face was turned slightly, and his hair messed and wet where his mother had wiped the grime from his forehead. Silently, he continued to watch as they wound his body in a winding sheet, covering his face, and tightened by a knot under his chin.

His mother Margery and her cousin knelt beside the body and clasped their hands together in unison, later joined by relatives, neighbours, and friends who guarded the corpse throughout the night. Two candles flickered, the shadows dancing on the black cloth that donned the walls. There they would remain until the vicar from Saint Michael and All Angels' chapel arrived to administer last rites and sprinkle holy water.

They would bury him on the grounds of Saint Michael and All Angels; however, as much of the church's land had been acquired by the noble right of King Henry VIII, and distributed to the wealthy, ground space was in shortage. An older grave site would be dug up, the bones removed, and there his father would be placed.

After his father had passed, the copy-hold inheritance of the hide automatically passed to Thomas being the eldest son; his mother attended the manor court in Haworth with him. All the other freeholders and copyholders tenanted to his lordship would be there also. Here, his tenancy would be accounted for and recorded on the Haworth manor court roll of Martin Birkhead, Esquire, as a proof of the right to the tenancy. He would swear an oath to Lord Birkhead, lord of the manor of Haworth, in exchange for yearly labouring services on his lands to the south-east of Haworth, a patch of non-arable land called Hall Green.

They left after the day's work, digging in the horse manure and human faeces, made harder by the constant drizzle. This valuable fertilizer had been collected over the course of the winter. They walked through the furrowed fields a dog barked in the distance, past the manor house at the foot of Main Street with its large cut ashlar gritstone and deeply recessed mullioned windows. The manor stood out in all its splendour amongst the nearby cruck houses. They walked up, up, up Sun Street, muddied and slippery underfoot.

The cottage merchants along the road sold all manner of items, from vegetables to wimples, but they were in the process of packing up for they too had to attend the court. They looked over the expanse of open Pennine countryside and moorlands on one side of the road. The sun was going down and cast shadows from trees on the other. The church tower of Saint Michael and All Angels was a continual reminder of the distance and steepness of the climb to the square.

CHAPTER 3

ROUGH TOUCH

Arriving outside their destination, mother ushered Thomas inside; they were both wet, feet muddied from the road. 'Go on Thomas, go on inside; we don't wanna get the payne of two shillings for bein' absent. Let the steward know who you are, and you're taking your father's tenure at Hall Green.'

Thomas ducked his head going through the doorway and was immediately stunned by the sharpness of the smell, urine-soaked straw and rotting food that had been thrown or dropped on the muddy, manure-covered floor. A man stumbled with a toilet bucket spilling more over the sides than what he was putting in. He tried at drunken modesty when he saw Margery, turning toward the wall to save embarrassment.

Another used a form as a bed, face down, still clinging to the almost empty Jack, lightly held for a future swig before staggering home. The window had no glass and shutters kept out the evening air, which on some nights, depending on the way of the wind, rid the room of the layers of smoke. The shutters also served the purpose of denying the vicar's representative, who occasionally walked by, to collect notes on the immoral goings on after dark. Three-legged stools and the odd cut barrel were used as a gaming table. Wide, rough planks rested on full size-barrels separating the barkeeper from the clientele and shelves behind housed pewter dishes, leather jacks and the odd pewter tankard for the patron with a more modest income. Most of the light came from the fire in the hearth, but the odd tallow candle chandelier and grease lamp provided enough light for the card games, arguments and political debates. The serving wench tracked backwards and forwards, replacing empty jacks with full ones for the patrons, on occasion disappearing upstairs for more physical pursuits and monetary gain.

One individual sat almost semi-conscious on his stool, head leaning back against the wall, red woolen hat pushed up. A vomit stain donned his tunic and dripped to the earthen floor. Two others looked on, whispering, and sizing him up, no doubt debating percentages of their share of his winnings, Thomas thought.

Both wore a black slouch hat which shadowed their face. No doubt strangers, as they were dressed more notably than the rest of the patrons. One had a black eye patch, which made him look more mysterious. He had on a red sheepskin doublet done up with a whole row of buttons lined from neck to waist, and a tan overcoat was placed on the stool beside him. A thick black belt wrapped around a sword leant against the wall near where they were sitting. The other, a slightly bigger man, held his sword, instinctively looking at his partner then around the room to try to gain truths from the expressions on the local's faces.

They were a ragtag bunch of tinkers, peasants and yeomen in from the weather, hiding from the wrath of their lord and their wives if they knew they weren't pushing the plough. The steward noticed the young lad and the old wench that walked through the door. He assumed they were there to pay the payne, fines or dues.

The drunkard, who they had come to know as John Hargreaves, was a mess and the two strangers were annoyed that he had so easily parted them from the steward's coin. They were even more annoyed that the steward had not told them of the demon dog from Stanbury who had killed so many rats. If they were to be working the territory for him, they would need to ensure better disclosure from the steward in the future.

They had met Hargreaves at the rat baiting and although a cheap drunk, had been generous with his celebrations. They watched patiently as he used the steward's coin to purchase half the tavern a round of ale.

Fortunately, they were not there to make a profit for the steward.

Margery elbowed him, 'There he is Thomas, the steward, sitting yonder playing the card game. Nip on over and let him know who you are.'

'No mother, not before the manor court,' replied Thomas nervously, not really knowing how to address the situation.

He had been to the manorial court once before with his father, before he died, but that was some time ago when he was only a young lad. His mother had castigated his father for taking him, saying it was a house of ill-repute and her sons would not be subjected to such a place. He remembered his father shrugging his shoulders and arguing the benefits of the excursion and how it would prepare his sons for future responsibility. His father had been greeted with many silent nods. How he had beamed with pride as he introduced his two sons to those nearby.

Impatiently, she led Thomas toward the table, 'Go on now, make thy self-known before someone else gets in before us 'n takes our hide.'

The steward was dressed in tight breeches, a short blue waistcoat of desirable fabric with sleeves reaching to just above the elbow. He wore a white ruffled long-sleeved shirt, cravat, and a ribbon dragged over one shoulder. His baggy black coat reached just above the knees and met with the tight stockings and garter. His thick leather shoes were polished and shone in the candlelight. He had an air of dignity, but the hidden importance of his office was not about him as he looked at his cards and the eyes of his companions.

Straight, long, black hair framed his face, thinned eyebrows, a thin black moustache and a small, triangular nest of hair sat below his bottom lip, which brought nobility to his full face. A man of medium build, but those hands, they hadn't done a day's work, almost like marble extensions of his arms.

He looked at his cards and tried to read the eyes of his companions, but was aware of Thomas' presence and the old wench that accompanied him. He also knew of the drunkard that was going to be left penniless in a ditch that night if he wasn't careful. He always liked to come to the Kings Arms early to see who was cheating at the games, like these two non-locals were. They probably did the rounds, Keighley, Oakworth, Oxenhope, Stanbury; making a good living from unsuspecting folk who knew no better. They apparently didn't spend any of their hard-earned winnings on their dress, for they looked ragged and worn, he thought to himself.

The cards depicted the countries of England and Wales, but he knew that the card's lime complexion hid the distinguishing mark somewhere in the textual description or inner frame. Nobody, he thought, could be that lucky.

His recently hired deputies would meet him at eight o'clock and by that time his companions would have won all of his coin and he would have them. He didn't like outsiders coming to town to take advantage of his people; he liked that monopoly for himself. The steward organised the rat baiting to coincide with the manor court for just that reason.

The steward had an inkling that the lord knew of his small pastime but allowed him to go unperturbed just as long as it did not cause disharmony among residents of the parish. The steward liked the extra shillings it brought in to supplement his income, primarily when the dog was 'on' and the owner, that he brought up from Stanbury, was right in his judgment of the number of rats. Of course, this was all calculated and controlled with the number of dried herbs he put in his feed. He knew that some in the village won and some lost; all that mattered to him was that he was at an advantage.

'I'm terribly sorry, but gentlemen, you are very fortunate tonight. I'm afraid one's luck is at an end. You have emptied my pocket,' said the steward, dropping his head disappointedly.

'It's alright your grace. We can take cash or goods. What about your pretty gold ring?' replied the other player. Another whispered and smiled with a toothless grin having already raised the stakes and bowed out of the game. They were unlikely men, the steward thought, especially Archie, the one with no teeth. He had an enormous nose that was continually running, which he regularly wiped on his sleeve. A faded red baggy cap tilted slightly, and a continual toothless smile added to his peculiarity. His dirty red, straw-like hair bristled from below his cap. He continually licked his lips and swallowed as if he always had too much saliva, spraying some of it when he tried to enunciate certain words. His companion's shirt attracted most of the spray, which wet the linen and blossomed into small wet patches that dotted his arm and shoulder.

The steward heard the call of the night watchmen from down the street, 'Sleep well ta thy locks, fire 'n thy leet, 'n God give theur grand night for now the bell rings eight.' Which was followed by the customary eight rings of the bell.

It was a chilly spring evening, and the drizzle was constant, keeping the soiled roads muddy and the thatched roofs damp.

The sun was setting, and the only light emanated from the candles in the small cottages down Main Street.

Further away, the night watchmen called out again, then continued down the road. He would be awake most of the night watching for strangers that might carry the sickness from York. If approached, he was under orders to refuse their passage and had the will and the weapons to enforce it. It wouldn't be the first time that a stranger found himself the lodger of the night watchman and his wife in the lock-up on North Street.

'You have won many shillings. How about one more hand? Goodness me,' he said as he took the gold ring from his small finger and placed it on top of the coinage in the middle of the table.

The toothless one quickly picked up the ring and bit it with one of his last remaining teeth at the side of his mouth. He nodded and placed the ring back on top of the pile, snickering with a foul cackle as he peeked at his companion's hand.

'Alright then your grace, we will give you one more chance to win thy coin back, but don't go complaining to the night watchman or the old steward if you lose,' Archie replied confidently as he looked again at his partner Stuart's cards.

The steward wiped a small droplet of spittle that had made its way to the back of his hand with his handkerchief. 'Indomitably not. One is a gentleman after all!'

The steward placed his cards face up on the top of the half barrel.

The toothless one's sadistic smile grew, and he let out another foul cackle as Stuart placed the winning hand down on the surface. 'Well your grace, it seems like the night were ours,' he said as he reached over to grab the gold ring.

The steward slammed his fist down on the top of the poor old boy's hand, cracking a finger in the process.

His voice turned deeper, and he stood knocking over his chair. 'SIMPLETONS, I AM A GENTLEMAN AND THE STEWARD, NOW GET READY TO PAY THY DEBT!'

The toothless one, with fear and shock in his eyes ran toward the door colliding with Thomas. 'GET OUT OF THE WAY FOOL!'

The culprit was knocked backwards over the sleeping man's form and into the arms of the steward's deputy who had been lingering near the bar.

He was a big man and picked his quarry up off the floor by the scruff of the neck. The toothless one's dirty cloth slippers started running in mid-air, trying to get purchase on the earthen floor. Spittle was firing from his mouth and dribble cascaded down his chin; his hat had fallen off, showing a large bald patch on the top of his head sided by wispy, red hair.

'LET ME GO YOU SOD, LET ME GO, YOU HAVE NO RIGHT!' said the captive as he struggled to remove the deputy's hands from the back of his tunic.

Thomas, albeit stunned by the goings on, remained unharmed and apologetic, believing he had wronged the stranger. He looked for his mother through the mayhem that had occurred. He saw her, lonesome on a stool near the hearth; warmed by the fire she was oblivious to the goings on and worried about the keeping of the hide.

'LET ME GO YOU VERMIN! I HAVEN'T DONE ANYTHING!' Archie yelled, trying to hit the deputy with backward swinging arms that missed and slowed as his collar was squeezed tighter. Then his arms went limp beside him like a rag doll.

'Relax yourself coney-catcher; thy work is done here,' said the deputy, who had the situation well under control.

He walked him over to a stool and plonked him down, then bound his hands with shackles roughly while his captive tried to struggle out. The toothless one quickly stood and tried to take a step until the deputy put his rather large hand on his shoulder and pushed him back down onto the stool. He tried to stand again. The deputy, slowly losing patience, put his hand on the top of his head and forced him back down unapologetically. He sat there with a glum look on his face, wiping his runny nose on the sleeve of his upper arm. He stared at Thomas, lifted his thumb to his neck, and dragged it across his throat. Thomas was shocked by his gesture.

Some in the room heard the word coney-catcher and whispered the news until everyone knew that there were tricksters thereabout. The crowd started to gather around, pointing and calling out obscenities to the two men who looked glum and disappointed.

The steward sat back down but grabbed Stuart's wrist as he reached for the winnings. 'I will take that, coney-catcher!'

The other deputy grabbed his wrists and shackled them quickly, shoving him over to sit on the stool beside his partner.

The steward scraped the rest of the winnings into his money purse, raising his eyebrows with a look of satisfaction. 'Seems like the night were mine after all.'

Stuart looked at the steward, hoping for leniency, then down at the ground with a look of despair and regret. Stuart thought of the events that had led to his predicament. He thought of his wife and children back in York and the hardship they had endured these past weeks. He remembered his wife, who had taken ill with the sickness. First there were the pockmarks on the legs, the fever, head pain, and then the lumps in the groin and under the armpits the size of an egg. He didn't have resources to pay for doctors, then once the body collectors found out, the red 'X' was painted on the door. That was the end of it. With sadness in his heart, he covered her with a linen sheet and allowed them to take her away to the mass grave on the outskirts of town. Fearing for his children, he smuggled them out of the house to his brother's, on the edge of town. Unfortunately, a day later they were bitten with the same symptoms and were also carted away. He knew he wasn't a bad man, but desperate times called for desperate measures and his toothless acquaintance's plan to flee the sickness and earn easy coin seemed like a good idea at the time.

As the steward stood, the publican and his helpers placed tables together for the twelve, the apostles that would determine the fate and future of many on the night. The steward sat and the twelve jurors approached and took their seats, led by the reeve of the manor who was the intermediary between the villagers and the lord.

The reeve was from a good family, voted to his position by the villagers each year to represent them and to evenly distribute responsibilities of labour to be carried out on the lord's demesne.

Yarns about the coney-catching were the topic of the night, especially what punishment the toothless one and his companion would get for their trickery at cards. The two men sat on their stools, hands shackled, faces forlorn, looking to the floor and quietly whispering ideas for their defense.

By this time the room was packed, the light from the tallow candles highlighted the layers of smoke which separated the floor to rafters. All eyes were on the two culprits, who sat nervously awaiting the next stage of their ordeal.

'HEAR YEE HEAR YEE, THE HAWORTH MANOR COURT IS NOW IN SESSION. ALL WHO HAVE BUSINESS ON THIS NIGHT COME FORWARD AND BE RECOGNISED!' yelled the deputy confidently.

Thomas looked at his mother who was standing near the fire. She gestured for him to walk forward toward the table.

The steward rose from his chair, an experienced orator, 'Eh up people of Haworth! The first case involves these cheeky two who thought me a rabbit for their stew. These cony-catchers, these vultures, these fatal harpies that putrefy with their infections in the flourishing estate of England. What say you?'

The occupants of the room, ale in hands and a touch tipsy, jostled for a good vantage point. They were aroused by the steward's words and started to yell obscenities.

'He emptied me pockets this evening, he did. HANG THEM!' yelled one disgruntled individual who sparked a call-in unison from many of the others.

'YEA HANG THE BASTARDS!' they all screamed.

'Hang the bastards and let no citizen of Haworth fall foul to these two again,' yelled another.

The two sat nervously watching and started to worry about their fate. 'They can't hang us, it's the first time we been caught,' whispered the toothless one as he wiggled and discreetly tried to free himself from his bonds.

Stuart, sitting beside him, quietly accepted his fate. 'Oh shut up. We should have left when I said so earlier,' he exclaimed.

Being argumentative, 'How was I to know he was the damn steward? We'll plead insanity that'll get us off it has before.'

The steward continued, 'Even though hanging would be a fitting punishment for these putrid two, they still have their ears and have not been scarred by previous misdeeds. What do you say in thy defense?' The steward pointed towards the two men.

'Insanity drove us to do it. Times are tough in York and our little ones have no food. PLEASE HAVE MERCY!' yelled Archie, looking at his companion for support.

'INSANITY, what say you?' The steward looked at the twelve jurors, who turned to each other and whispered, gesticulating, nodding and shaking their heads in disproval.

As they hushed, one of the twelve, the reeve from the manor, stood representing the group. 'CAUGHT RED HANDED WITH

MARKED CARDS, we say a day on the pillory and finally to be released into God's hands with the lopping of the right ear.'

Some patrons cheered as others booed, missing out on a good hanging; however, they knew that even though there would be no hanging, they could still have their retribution while the culprits were on public display.

'NOOOO, NOOOO, PLEASE 'AVE MERCY, our wee ones starve if were absent!' screamed Archie. 'IT WERE HIS IDEA, NOT MINE TAKE HIM' He stood and pointed to his companion.

The deputy once again forced his shoulder downward for a seat on the stool. His companion, somewhat shocked, looked up at him silently, then at the crowd, who had become even more excited by the thought of the coming punishment.

The steward rose, and the crowd settled for the verdict. 'THE FOLK OF HAWORTH HAVE SPOKEN! Take them to the pillory and let the locals decide their fate over the next day. Let it be known that the citizens of Haworth will not be the victims of coney-catchers any longer. TAKE THEM AWAY!'

The steward could have hanged them, but he knew the difference between punishment for hanging and punishment for thieving and questions would be asked by the justice of the peace if the sentence did not fit the crime.

The deputies took the scoundrels by their shackles out into the night air, followed by the rabble, who lit the way with candles seized from the alehouse, covering them to shield them from the drizzle. They sloshed through the mud of the square to the pillory, which was set outside the rocky made steps to Saint Michael and All Angels Church, a reminder to all who might be caught on the wrong side of the law.

Hearing the commotion, the vicar and his offsider appeared with a torch. 'Who goes there?' he called out as he lifted the torch to get a glimpse of the crowd that disturbed him.

The mob were not used to seeing the vicar out of his usual Sunday regalia. 'Putting coney-catchers on the pillory vicar. Caught red-handed, they were. Steward has sentenced them to three days,' said the deputy.

The vicar, not wanting to get involved in the village's business, lifted his two fingers piously. 'God save you.' He turned and hurriedly walked back to the church out of the drizzle.

In the wooden framework with holes for the head and hands, the toothless one and the player were unceremoniously placed. The deputy forcing their head and hands into curves of the frame, closing, latching and replacing the old, rusted lock. Then the other deputy took a large four-inch nail and placed it at the top of the player's outstretched ear. He took a wooden handled hammer and struck home four times, sending the nail through the ear deeper and deeper into the wood behind. The small crowd cheered in unison each time the hammer struck the nail. The player screamed, his face contorted with the pain, blood dripping down the side of his face and off the bottom of the frame. He whimpered from the sting as the shock took hold.

The toothless one continued to plead his innocence, once again trying to divert blame to his companion and promote sympathy for his young ones that had not been fed.

'HAVE MERCY! I will leave Haworth and not return. I SWEAR IT! have mercy…' His last word was cut short as the deputy made the first blow on the nail head, through the ear cartilage into the timber behind.

The crowd cheered 'AYYYE… AYYYE… AYYYE' After each stroke of the hammer and then laughed, some hysterically having never witnessed such exciting entertainment before.

Archie screamed, swallowed and screamed again, tears in his eyes, 'YOU SON OF A WHORE, I will have all of you one day, I swear it! Your wife, your young ones, will never be safe. They will spend their days lookin' over their shoulder.' His hands trembled, and his matted, wet hair stuck to his face. Droplets of blood dribbled down the wooden frame and dripped, to be diluted by the constant drizzle on the ground below him.

The deputy smiled wickedly, walked around the back of the frame and placed a well-aimed kick between his legs. 'Oh SHUT UP you insignificant fopdoodle!' he bellowed. He then raised his head to the sky and roared with a deep belly laugh, feeling good about his dealings and insult.

The crowd cheered and laughed as the toothless one grimaced in pain and shrieked as he felt the pain in his ear as it ripped a little. The discomfort moved from his ear to between his legs, but it was a different type of pain and his breath was knocked from his chest and felt like his testicles would rise into the cavity of his empty stomach.

Blood mixed with his long dirty reddish coloured hair and started to congeal on the side of his face. 'COP THAT YOU! That'll teach ya' not to come diddling Haworth grand folk,' as one of the men stepped forward and spat in his face.

The ale flavoured phlegm clung to his face and slowly dribbled down his cheek to rest in the corner of his open mouth. His lips quivered as he frustratedly tried to squeeze his hands through the holes in the frame.

One of the other onlookers picked up a handful of mud, squashed it into a ball, then threw it at Stuart hitting him square in the side of the face. A small blotch of red emanated from his skin from the concealed stone. The crowd cheered as the rain came down harder. Having their fill of insults, they all returned quickly to the alehouse to warm themselves by the fire and leave the toothless one and his companion to the ravages of the night.

The two were left in the dark to ride the pain and discomfort of the last few minutes. The rabble followed the dwindling candle back across the square and back into the Kings Arms to await the next order of business.

Archie groaned, 'They'll pay for this, I swear, ALL OF 'EM WILL PAY! ESPECIALLY THE BOY!'

While they were away, the steward had dealt with and fined one who had allowed his cattle to stray onto the lord's demesne. He had also dealt with and received payment from a freeman who wanted to dispute the erection of a fence by his neighbour. They both accepted the payne. One for erecting the fence without the lord's blessing and the other for knocking part of the fence down without the lord's blessing. The steward also took coin from a man and woman who had engaged in pre-marital sex, and as such, were bound together forever. All monies collected of course went to the lord's coffers to keep him in the luxury that he was used to. Well, all except a small portion that the steward and the clerk skimmed for themselves.

The door opened and Thomas and his mother watched the rabble make their way back into the room. They were quick to report the goings-on that had occurred outside, especially the treatment of the toothless one at the hands of the big deputy. The deputies returned to the side of the steward who was ready to call business to an end and return to his penny ale.

One last time he stood. 'Is there any more business? If so, say it now or forever hold thy peace.' Looking around the room, he noticed the old wench pushing Thomas forward through the crowd.

CHAPTER 4

TRUTH OF A BOY

The steward looked at Thomas and the woman, as Thomas took off his hat as a sign of respect. 'What say theur lad? It is getting late and I must return to the hearth of my fire, speak up now or let it hold on for three weeks until the next court.'

'Ah'm sorry your grace, my mother and I, it is our first court and we don't rightly know the way of proceedings as it were normally my father who attended,' Thomas spoke quietly.

'Speak up lad, where is thy father? Lest he receive a fine for nonappearance's sake,' said the steward, trying to obtain more coin.

Thomas and his mother stood there nervously with most of the occupants looking at them and whispering words of sadness for the passing of his father, who they all knew to be a man of integrity. They all agreed he was the first to help if anybody was behind with the harvest and leant a hand with the ploughing of destitute families if they needed it.

Meanwhile, the deputy leaned over and whispered in the steward's ear. The steward raised his ear and listened intently. A short time later, he looked at Thomas and his mother showing a hint of sympathy.

While Thomas was waiting for the steward, he looked down at his foot coverings, covered in mud, a small hole starting to wear at the top near his big toe. His tunic was soaked, and he could feel his undershirt clinging to his back. Thomas fiddled with a piece of straw, trying to remove it from the attached mud on his foot. He could feel the dampness of his hose attached to his legs, sagging and loosened by the weight of the wet.

'I'm sorry to hear about thy father lad, God rest his soul. You are here ta pay the death payment to Lord Birkhead, are you not? Pay the shilling to the clerk and let the night's business be done lad,' said the steward, growing increasingly anxious and although sympathetic, had other things on his mind.

Apologetically, Thomas muttered, 'We don't have any coin yer grace, last coin went to pay for the funeral.'

Starting to lose his patience, the steward retorted, 'Neya coin? Then why are you here? Blast us.'

He looked up at the deputy hoping for an explanation; the deputy shrugged his shoulders in earnest, not knowing what to say.

The steward turned to his clerk. 'Make a note clerk, the Rushworth family of Hall Green have not paid for the father's funeral.'

The clerk sitting on the other side of the table, with a small candle shedding light, took a quill, dipped it in the small jar of ink and wrote on his ledger carefully. He knew how the lord liked to look at his incomings and outgoings on a regular basis and risked a severe scolding if it was not legible.

The deputy leaned down again and whispered something in the steward's ear.

The steward grunted, nodded, and looked at Thomas. 'My deputy tells me you were of some assistance ta him this evenin' when the culprit that currently holds up the pillory with his right ear tried to escape. In that case, then we are in debt ta thee lad. What is it you want from us?'

Sheepishly, Thomas looked at his mother, then back at the steward. 'Just ta keep our tenancy at Hall Green for his lordship, as did my father, 'n his father before him.'

The steward looked about the room, which had quietened. He called out to the twelve jurors, 'Can anybody here about provide any reason why this young man should not continue to be the copyholder on his

Lord's tenancy at Hall Green? If so, speak now!'

The jurors looked at one another.

The reeve stood and everybody hushed. 'I have known young Rushworth since he were a baby still at his mother's breast. He's a hard worker like his father was. He'll do a grand service to his lordship.'

The reeve looked at Thomas proudly, having known the family for many years and still remembered the support of his father when the voting for his position came around each year.

The steward stood speaking quietly, 'Reeve, has the family heard the divine service and do they attend regularly?'

'They have yer grace.'

'Then it is settled. His lordship will expect a portion of grain from your next harvest and each one after that. As copyholder and tenant of Hall Green, you swear oath to Lord Birkhead of Haworth Manor in exchange for yearly labouring services. Make thy mark on the court roll as proof of tenancy.' He pointed to the clerk.

Thomas swore his oath on the King James Bible and made an X with the quill pen handed to him. He and his mother bowed then turned toward the door sighing in relief. Thomas pushed his way through the watching crowd, making space for his mother. Respectfully, the crowd parted and allowed Mrs Rushworth and Thomas to walk unheeded.

'Sorry ta hear about ol' Thomas, Mrs,' called out one man.

'Yer, sorry to hear. He was a fine bloke,' said another.

It was late. Thomas and his mother made their way out into the night air with an oil rag torch she had left at the door. They walked across the muddy square and down Sun Street. The drizzle had finally abated and Thomas, protectively holding the arm of his mother, who by this time had her share of the penny ale and found the muddy road even more slippery than usual. Down past the roadside cottages they went, eventually reaching the be-speckled candle lights of the manor. The household dogs barked and growled but were tempered by their handler who patrolled the property.

The dog handler, hearing their footsteps trudging through the mud, called out, 'Who goes there? Be you bonnie lad or foe, say thy name, as my dog does not care.'

'It is Thomas and Margery Rushworth yer grace, tenants of his lord from Hall Green returning home from manor court.'

'I have heard of the goings on in the court, 'tis a lousy night. Be careful going home for there's a foul mist,' his voice quietened with the parting distance they walked.

A dog barked across the beck and the moon provided some light to guide them. The wind picked up force across the moorlands, the Pennine all but covered in a ghost-like mist. They walked across the fallow field and made their way up the side of the strip of land they tended from dawn to dusk. Sheep, like white marauders, looked up disinterested as they grazed on land that had once been tenanted by other families like theirs, now divided by dry stone walls.

They saw him face down in the ditch at the side of the field, one leg bent awkwardly across the other, his shirt sodden from the earlier drizzle, and there was no movement. As they drew closer and lowered the torch, Thomas noticed a bloodied gash on the back of his head matted and congealed with blood. There was no sound except the rustling of the heather and a quiet groan coming from the injured man.

Thomas got closer and lightly placed his hand on the man's back. Margery warned him not to get involved.

'We can't leave him mother. The beasts will have him through the night. He still breathes.'

'Aye, and if you get the blame for this and end up hanging from a rope, what are we to do?' she replied worriedly as she looked up at the light coming from their cottage.

'Come on mother, help me get him up, and we'll take him back to ours.' Thomas passed the torch to his mother.

'These are dangerous times son, what if he's Catholic? Leave him be fer God's sake.'

Thomas dragged him out of the ditch, lifted one arm and heaved him onto his shoulder; the stranger groaned. Thomas was unsteady on his feet, so he took the first step carefully. He could feel the mud move underneath his feet; he took another, his mother placed her hand on the small of his back to steady him.

'I can smell spew!' he exclaimed while grimacing from the smell and the dead weight.

Margery walked slightly ahead, lighting the way grumbling as she went. It wasn't far now, the light from the fire could be seen through the cracks in the shutters. Margery could see that William had already brought the animals in and was probably in bed half asleep.

'WILLIAM HELP US!' yelled Margery.

Groggily, William jumped up from his straw mattress. The dogs barked, causing a commotion inside. As Margery got closer to the cottage, the dogs growled and made for the front door. Growling and barking, they paced the width of the door, trying to look underneath to get a glimpse of the unfamiliar scent.

'WILLIAM IT'S US OPEN THE DOOR. We need help, hold the dogs back 'cause we have a guest,' Margery yelled.

'GEW WAY DOGS.' William shooed them away, so they moved to the other side of the hearth. They both stood, curious about the scent. One of them started to move closer, the other behind him. They were agitated and alert, tongues protruding, their large black sagging lips drooling in anticipation. Tan, large muscular chest and hindquarters, solidly built with a huge snout and black ears, they were fine specimens. Affectionate and, of course, protective.

As William opened the door, Thomas came bustling in, exhausted by the weight on his shoulder. The dogs barked and sniffed at the dangling hand. As carefully as he could, he laid the stranger down on the floor and straightened to relieve the pain in his back. The dogs nervously sniffed and retreated as the stranger groaned. Then they returned to continue their investigation, sniffing and then licking the vomit stain on his tunic. One sniffed his crotch; the other stood near his face, looking up toward Thomas, drooling. A line of saliva slowly dangled, then dropped onto the stranger's face.

'Gew way dog.' Thomas shooed them away to the back of the room.

'What are you doin' brother? Bringin' a corpse to our home,' said William. 'Have we not more important things to contend with here.'

'Quiet William, he's not dead. He fell afoul of the night and needed our help!'

'Our help? The only help he needed was another ale. Look at the state of him.'

The dog's inquisitiveness, now half abated by familiarity, started to develop again as they sniffed at the stranger's nether regions. A release of foul stench emanated from his britches and after one inhale, the dogs decided they didn't want another and turned away. Still curious, they decided to watch from further away. A wet, steamy shadow started to appear on his codpiece and spread. A pool grew under the cover of the straw meandering along the troughs and cracks of the earthen floor. Margery, smelling the foulness, reached for the wooden bucket of water needed for the family's night waste and flung it at the stranger's crotch.

Thomas turned him on his side and lifted his head, folding a small blanket for it to rest on, while Margery blotted the wound on the back of his head with a wet piece of linen. She washed it so that she could better see the wound. Parting the matted, damp hair, she squeezed the two pieces of skin together. More blood trickled from the wound and meandered its way down through his dark hair onto his neck, discolouring the collar of his undershirt.

When Margery let go of the wound it opened again and more blood escaped. 'William bring me my box with the thread and a needle.' She rinsed the cloth in the wooden bowl and once again blotted the wound to try to stop the flow of blood.

'Give me your knife Thomas.' She took the knife and cut away at the hair around the wound so that she could see better. She closed one eye and carefully threaded the needle with the thread that she used to mend clothes. She blotted the wound once again and squeezed the two pieces of skin together. Pushing the needle through the skin she trembled with effort as it was resistant. After it pierced, she grabbed the pointed end of the needle, which was halfway through and pulled the thread through tight, then repeated the action. Eventually, the two pieces of skin started to come together, and the flow of blood slowed. After finishing the last stitch she rinsed the cloth and blotted the wound one last time. Then ripping a strip of linen she tied it around his head.

'We'll let him rest here tonight, and he can be gone in the morning before any suspicions are raised,' whispered Margery.

Thomas turned. 'William, make a bed for him on the other side of the hearth. We'll stoke the fire and leave a candle burning in case he wakes during the night. Tomorra', I will nip on up and see the reeve.'

'No Thomas, tomorrow we will see him on his way in case his further presence curses us,' said Margery worriedly.

'She's right Thomas, we could be harbouring a Catholic fugitive fer all we know,' said William.'

With empathy in his eyes Thomas whispered, 'Mother, would you want to see me or William seen off if we were in a similar situation?'

Pausing, Margery looked up. 'Well son, God forbid, I would hope that you wouldn't be daft enough ta fall foul of the ale and be found face down in a ditch.'

'Let us talk no more about it tonight, let us sleep on it and see what the morning brings,' exclaimed Thomas as he looked down at the stranger.

'William, help me get him to the mattress.'

Margery and Thomas took the stranger's shoulders and William took the feet, laying him down on the straw mattress on the other side of the hearth as carefully as they could.

The stranger took shallow breaths and looked pale, his hose muddied and wet, clung to his legs. The dark stain on his tunic from the vomit was still apparent, but had started to lighten from the warmth of the fire. The sleeves of his undershirt were wet and soiled.

'I know something for sure, he's gonna have a rotten headache in the morning,' said William, smiling.

The dogs, annoyed by the stranger's presence at their hearth, took up their positions for the night, head on paws, eyes open, watching for any movement from the stranger.

Thomas and William climbed the ladder to the loft that hung over the far side of the cottage. The waste bucket was half filled with water and left at the bottom of the ladder where it could be easily found in the darkness of the night. Margery lifted her woolen kirtle, squatted and released a steady stream of steamy urine which flowed into the bucket. She smiled with contentment. As she relaxed her bowels, her flatulence escaped in a deep sounding long-running reverberation. The splash of her faeces could be heard. The dogs lifted their heads from their paws in a quizzical fashion and, realising what it was, put their heads back down and returned to their half slumber.

'Better out than in,' she declared, as she dipped her hand in the clean water bucket beside and wiped the residual. She grabbed the bottom of her kirtle, dried her hands, and tiredly ascended the ladder. After she had undressed, she took up her place on the straw mattress between the two boys. William was already reverberating a deep guttural sound from the back of his throat and Thomas was sound asleep.

༺

Thomas and William stirred with the rooster's call, woke before the birth of the sun and rose to the sound of their mother's complaining tone of voice.

Margery had already been awake for an hour; she didn't sleep much at night these days. Quietly, by the glow of the fading fire, she dressed in the kirtle that she had folded and left neatly at the bottom of the straw mattress and made her way down the ladder until she realised her wimple was missing. She climbed carefully back up to the loft, feeling around in the darkness near her mattress. She smiled touching her head, realising that it was still heir apparent. Feeling somewhat groggy from the previous night's penny ale, she quickly remembered the events that had transpired and looked sharply for evidence of their guest. *There he is, hasn't moved.*

Margery lifted her kirtle and began to squat on the bucket. There he was, hadn't moved, the dogs still wary and apprehensive about the stranger.

The male and female English mastiffs, although still puppies, were still a force to be reckoned with if the stranger had woken to take part in any misdeeds. Margery stoked the fire again and put two pieces of peat on the new flames. She stirred the pottage and opened the door for the dogs to relieve themselves. They hesitated, looking at the open door and then back at the stranger.

'Gew on dogs, he means no harm, go and do thy business,' she said, shooing them out the door.

While leading the cow toward the door, it lifted its tail and released a stream of excrement which landed on the floor in the shape of a steaming patty. The cow's udder was full and needed milking, but she would tend to the water and the pottage first.

The two sheep and lamb followed through the opening, happy to nibble at the long grass around the cottage. She took the cow to the common green and pegged its long rope to the ground to keep it from wandering onto his lordship's demesne.

Thomas was already making his way down the ladder, partly dressed but not ready for the day. Some of his hair stood on end and his eyes were still not fully open. When he got to the bottom, he turned and raised his arms, stretching his muscles and his back to wake and loosen the stiffness. His back cracked, he lowered his arms, reached into his codpiece and gave his right testicle a scratch. He unlatched his codpiece and relieved himself in the bucket, the aroma from Margery's previous night's contribution wafting up his nose. He turned his face, but too late to save his nostrils from the acrid stench. He gave it a shake and put it back in his codpiece, then called out to William who was still in bed.

'WILLIAM GET OUT OF BED, the day is born and there is work to be done.'

William, accustomed to being last out of bed, sat up and started rubbing the sleeping grit from his eyes. 'I was having a dream, a beautiful dream about a lass, hair of gold, eyes as blue as the sky on a bright spring day.'

'Yer, well dream about your lass later, we 'ave work to do.'

William, partly dressed, his undershirt a hand-me-down from his brother and way too long, hung down to his knees. Annoyed, he stepped down the ladder slowly so as not to step on his shirt. He slowly pulled on his hose and attached his codpiece, then he turned, excited to see the stranger still in the same position where they left him the previous night.

'Do ya' think he's alive, brother?'

'I heard him groan before and he turned his face from the fire.'

'What if he's a Catholic Recusant? We could get in all types of shite.'

'Watch yer tongue in this house William. Save thy father a trip back from the grave ta give you a hiding.'

'It's no business of ours William, whether he is or he isn't,' replied Thomas.

All the time the stranger had been listening with his eyes closed. *Who are these people? Where am I? Erggh my head hurts!*

Margery went outside, picked up the yoke, the wooden crosspiece that held the buckets, and placed it on her shoulders to make her way to Bridgehouse Beck about half a mile away. She would make three trips during the day to ensure water for the animals, the waste bucket, the washing of clothes, and water for the ale.

Through the wheat fields she went, past the cottages, across Sun Street, through the trees and down the hill. She could hear the movement of the water cascading down the small waterfall near her favourite collection point. She was careful walking down the bank, still damp from the morning dew. The sun had started to rise, and it glistened through the leaves of the trees like glistening diamonds. She put the yoke on the ground and then rubbed her shoulder where the wood had dug into her and made its mark. The pebbles from the beck crunched underfoot as she bent down to fill one bucket, then the other.

She hitched the two buckets and straightened her back under the weight of the watery load, being careful not to spill any. The journey home was a lot slower. She took her time going up the hill and paused halfway up, out of breath.

Thomas walked over to the table in the corner under the loft and filled the wooden basin with fresh water from a bucket. He splashed his face, his chest and under his arms, pushing his wet hands through his dark hair, grimacing from the shock of the cold water. Thomas cupped his hand, held in his stomach and poured some water down the inside front of his hose. He quickly washed the front and back of his nether regions, repeating the routine until he was satisfied that all was cleaner, and he had removed the louse and bed bugs that liked to congregate and leave their mark at night-time.

By this time Margery had returned with the water, she added some corn, wheat, and beans to the pottage and stirred and scraped the sides of the cauldron. The aroma filled the room and filled the nostrils of the stranger that started to stir. He groaned, the dogs growled, he lifted his head, opened one eye and collapsed back down onto the straw mattress, the previous night's events a muddled memory.

William knelt beside him with a leather jack of ale. 'Sip this my friend, have the hair of the dog that bit thee.'

The stranger leant on his elbow and grimaced in pain as he felt the dried knot of blood on the back of his head. 'Where am I lad? I know not.'

'Hall Green, not far from Haworth manor. We found you in a ditch at the bottom of the hide and brought you home ta sleep it off. We didn't know if you would wake today,' replied Thomas.

John Hargreaves wasn't to know, but this kind act was to have a profound effect on the rest of his and his family's future.

William looked over, empathising with the stranger while Margery spooned some pottage into bowls. 'Leave the poor soul son, let him rest and greet the day in a bit.'

The stranger groggily sat up from his straw mattress, clutching the back of his head. The dogs stood and growled.

'SILENCE DOGS, HEEL!' yelled Thomas.

The dogs dropped to the floor once again, but still maintained a vigilance.

Margery handed the stranger a bowl of pottage and a wooden spoon, 'Get that into ya', give ya' strength for the journey home.'

'Do you remember what happened?' enquired Thomas.

'I remember winning at the rat baiting. I remember celebrating and drinking ale with two men. Not locals. I hadn't seen them before. The alehouse wench kept fetching more and more ale and I kept buying. The last I remember was walking down the street with my companions on the way home.'

'Do you remember what they looked like?' asked Thomas.

'They were dressed different. They had swords and one had a patch on his eye.'

'I remember them,' said Thomas excitedly.

'I must be on me way, I thank you for your hospitality. My name is John Hargreaves and I live near Moorehouse Lane toward Oxenhope. I better be off before my wife 'n daughter Agnes believe I've left this mortal world.'

'If there's anything I can do to repay you, me hide is on the way to Oxenhope. I have neighbours thereabouts and my daughter serves his Lordship at Haworth Manor. I am forever in thy debt, don't know what would have happened if you hadn't come along.'

'Take more pottage and ale before you go Mr Hargreaves,' Margery said while spooning more pottage into his bowl.

Sitting on the stool by the fire, taking a sip from his bowl, Thomas swallowed and looked up. 'Will you report this to the steward, Mr Hargreaves?'

'That thieving bastard, he'd probably fine me for being drunk hereabouts. Bad enough I must pay the tithe to the church and the tax to the Lord. I don't want ta fill his pockets more than I have to, excuse the English, mother,' said John stubbornly.

'Nothing I haven't heard before,' exclaimed Margery as she took the empty bowls and started to wash them in the bucket of cold water. 'Right, I must be off then, I have ploughing to start and I'm late. The wife will not be happy. I was only supposed to walk Agnes home from the manor on a wicked night, but got waylaid by the goings on at manor court.'

'Next you are in the area, call in, think nothing of it,' said Thomas, shaking his hand as he stepped toward the door.

'Aye 'n next time, fetch your daughter Agnes with ya' too, let us meet the lass,' Margery said sheepishly while winking at Thomas.

Thomas opened the bottom half of the cattle door, the sun was rising. 'Safe journey my friend.'

'Tarreur Thomas, remember if there's anything you need.' John, being a bit disorientated, tried to get his bearings for home.

He wiped his forehead and tried to forget about the embarrassment from the previous night.

What a fine family, he thought to himself. He hadn't been treated so well by their kind before, but he wondered if they would have been so kind if they knew he was Catholic.

He remembered the problems they had faced before moving to Haworth and how he and his family had been persecuted in the last parish. Masses were banned, Catholic priests went missing presumed to be executed, and they were fined twelve pence each Sunday for not attending the king's Church of England. His wife Marg and his daughter Agnes faced a daily struggle of finger pointing, whispering and humiliation. He sometimes wondered if it was all worth it, especially for poor Agnes, who back then, didn't quite know what was going on and why they didn't go to church anymore. The poor dear couldn't understand why the other children wouldn't play with her and the songs they sang about her hurt.

He made his way across the ploughed fields to Sun Street past the broken dry wall, cottages on the left, rising hills dotted with sheep, on the right. Up the hill he went where it turned into Marsh Lane.

It was tough going, a morning chill; the dew made the muddy lane slippery, and he could feel the sweat oozing through his pores as he walked. There were green fields on both sides of the road and the sun was rising over his right shoulder; and the light hurt his eyes. He finally reached the top of the hill and let his wobbly legs carry him down the other side. He went past more cottages; most of the families already up and dragging the plough, some with oxen, others without. It seemed to take ages in his current state, but he was on the homeward stretch now, left on Moorhouse Lane, across the field and there it was, home at last.

The door was wide open, and his wife Marg was nowhere to be seen. He walked inside and warmed himself by the fire noticing the dark vomited stain on his tunic. His hose was damp, dirty and stained and his head hurt both inside and out. He took his shirt and hose off and left them in a pile near the fire. He walked to the ceramic water bowl and just as he splashed water on his face, she walked in, having just returned with buckets of water from Bridgehouse Beck.

She looked at his nakedness as he was bent over the bowl and smiled at his whiteness and knobby knees.

'Oh, there you are 'usband, Agnes was worried about you. Where have you been? Up to no good I suppose,' said his wife sarcastically.

'Careful wife, I don't need cheek this mornin' my head is split,' as John turned to show her the back of his head.

'Goodness John, what have you done?' asked his wife as she hurried to the kitchen and took a wet cloth to the back of John's head slowly cleaning it.

John grimaced in pain. 'My God wife, do you want ta open it up again? You don't know what'll come spilling out if you do.'

Stupid old fool. This is retribution for not going to church, I knew it would start again.

'No wife, it was footpads. They must have known that I had a purse full of winnings. I went to the Kings Arms for an ale. There were rat-baiting in the basement, so I wagered a shillin' or two and won.'

'Sounds like you won too much,' said his wife, lifting his tunic from the floor noticing the stain.

She looked at him curiously. 'And what may I pray have happened to the winnings?'

'Sorry wife, they are long gone. I woke up in a stranger's house with an empty money purse. I was found in a ditch on their hide and they took me home ta sleep off the wound,' he said apologetically, remembering the hospitality the Rushworth's had shown him.

'I'd say you were sleeping off more than the wound 'n besides, did you not think it might have been them that took the winnings?'

John condemned her accusation, 'No wife, it wasn't them. I was assaulted on the way home. If it wasn't for young Rushworth 'n his family, who knows what my fate would have been. They tended to the wound 'n put me near the fire, let me sleep it off while this morning, fed me pottage 'n gave me ale to wash it down with, no wasn't them. They are kind folk like us, but not of the faith.'

Margaret looked at him curiously. 'My goodness, now I've 'eard everything!'

John turned to her. 'They were different, kind and generous. The woman had two handsome lads, William and her eldest Thomas, about Agnes' age.

'They didn't know I was of the faith, but I get the feeling that it wouldn't have mattered.'

'Husband you don't know that. We must be careful; I don't want our Agnes to go through all that again. We must be silent and keep our prayers to ourselves. If it gets out that we're recusants, then it will all start again!' She sat down, put her face in her hands and sobbed.

'There, there, wife we'll be careful.' *She's a good woman and I hate to see her like this. I must remain steadfast and follow the true faith.*

John put his hand on Margaret's shoulder. 'It's alright wife, nobody will ever find us and I will continue to pay the fine for not attending church, but I refuse to a pray to a false God and that's that! Come now wipe yer eyes and let's talk no more about it.'

CHAPTER 5

SONS OF HEART

Thomas and William walked the mile to the manor to borrow two oxen and the suhl in exchange for a live chicken.

The reeve tended them out the back. It wasn't the first time they had been to the manor, but they were always impressed by its magnificence. Crushed stone carriageways, manicured grass and you could smell the fragrance of the roses tended so delicately to by the gardener. It always seemed to be a hive of activity, people coming and going, buying, selling and it was here that the reeve took care of business.

'This is all you have young Thomas, one chicken? The lord will be wanting more than that for your use.' The reeve glanced at the oxen. 'You want me to have to pay thy debts lad? I got me own family to tend to,' said the reeve busily while attending another visitor.

James had just finished weeding the Lord's top field and was bringing back the hoe. 'Ayup Jamey boy, do I have to go down and check,' the reeve called out, 'Last time you missed half the field.'

James kept walking toward the gate and quickened his pace, waving casually without turning around, obviously in a hurry to get back to his own cottage.

Young Jonathon had brought back the axe that his father used to cut wood in the forest for the lord's fire. 'Ayup young Jono, me boy, let me have a look at that blade, if it's not true you can stay and turn the grinding wheel awhile until it is,' the reeve said, lifting the axe and looking down the blade to see if there were any imperfections.

Continuing before Thomas could utter a word, 'And Thomas, I hear theur didn't pay the death payment at the manor court so you are in debt to the lord twice. I'd be careful lad, you don't want thy family thrown off the hide.'

'What work do you want to be done for the lord this week?' asked Thomas, knowing that it was customary to work three days for the lord on his demesne.

Thomas and his father, when he was alive, made the most of working for the lord. It was work, but they didn't toil as hard as they did on their own land. At times, they went fishing together to put trout on the lord's table; on other occasions they went into the forest and found mushrooms. Occasionally, father would hide a couple in his codpiece, and they would have them in the pottage that night. Another time, the reeve asked them to pick apples from the orchard. He remembered his father picking one, looking around to see if anybody was about, shining it on his tunic and then telling him to climb up the ladder into the top of the tree to eat it. Of course, if found out his father would have received a right flogging for it.

'Steward wants another dry bap wall built on the old Smithe hide, you can start that,' the reeve replied, waking young Thomas from his memories.

Thomas looked at the reeve angrily. 'Another pasture? Soon there won't be enough land ta feed any of us!'

'Well, if folk like you paid their dues, the lord would keep people rather than sheep. Now be off with ya' and don't forget the fine next time I see you or else I'll come looking for ya,' said the reeve impatiently. He knew that if the lord or steward found out about his generosity, it would come from his own purse.

As Thomas and William turned and walked away toward the oxen, the reeve called out, sympathy in his voice, 'Thomas, William, sorry about thy father, he were a grand man.'

He lifted the axe again to have another look and left the two lads to tend to the oxen and suhl.

Walking to the barn, Thomas looked across and noticed the steward; he was talking to the two strangers he recognised from the Kings Arms. They were both dressed well, likely men not of this village.

Clean mutton sleeves wide at the top tapering to the wrist. Their hose was clean, dry and tied at the knee with a garter. Swords hung in a sheath from the waist with a large black belt diagonally securing it. They wore fine leather shoes with a heel and a buckle like the steward.

Thomas looked at the shoes and then down at his own foot wrappings bunched at the top and covered in mud.

Thomas lifted his hand to shade the sun from his eyes. 'William, I recognise those men standing there. I saw them at the manor court, they were there when mother and I arrived.'

'So, you should brother, one of them is the lord's steward.'

While Thomas was looking over, the steward gave one of the men a small leather coin purse.

'How long will you be staying?' the steward asked.

'As long as it takes,' replied the man with the eyepatch.

The steward grinned. 'Well, I can put you to work while you're here and be my guests at the manor.' He didn't know them, but they seemed of high station.

'That is very kind of you, your grace.'

While sharing pleasantries, the steward noticed Thomas and his brother staring at them.

What are those two looking at? he thought. *They should keep out of other's business.*

The steward's smile turned to a frown. He shook hands with the two men, bid them farewell, and started walking toward Thomas and William.

William, worriedly, walked quicker toward the tied-up oxen. 'Christ, now you've done it. The stewards coming over here, let's get.'

Thomas dropped his head and quickened his pace. 'Let me do the talking brother,' as he arrived at the stall and started unhitching the oxen.

The steward approached, 'Ahh, Rushworth I believe, 'n what brings you to the manor, dear boy?' he asked in a demeaning tone.

The steward rarely spoke to the common folk unless it involved coin or payne at the manor court, preferring to leave that to the reeve.

'Just getting the oxen for the ploughing, sir,' Thomas took off his hat in a sign of respect.

Thomas and William dropped their heads in submission, they couldn't take their eyes off the steward's polished and buckled shoes.

'You seemed right interested in my companions before young Thomas. Do you know them? Is there anything you need to tell me?' asked the steward.

Thomas looked nervous and William didn't look. 'No, your grace, I were just admiring the manor gardens and thinking what a wonderful place it must be to live here,' he said.

At that point, the reeve came out the back door and came running over shouting, 'LORD WANTS TO SEE YOU YOUR GRACE!'

The steward turned, 'What does he want reeve?'

Thomas winked at William and took advantage of the distraction to lead the ox and head for home.

'STOP!' yelled the steward, convincing himself to continue with his questioning. He walked further to take up a position in front of them.

'Thomas, you did not take care of the payne, fines or dues at the manor court. Your father's funeral sum is still owing, and I hear you only paid a chicken for use of the oxen and suhl.'

Thomas took off his hat again and dropped his head in submission. He stood there patiently, waiting for the steward's next words. The steward leant forward so that nobody else, including William, could hear.

His breath had the aroma of ale, old port, garlic and onions, no doubt a tasty memory of last night's dinner with the lord, that from the smell, had been repeating on him all morning.

'Young Thomas, you should remember how grand Lord Birkhead has been to thee, allowing you to be a copyholder on his lands.

'You are lucky, and you should be right careful to not put thy nose in business that does not concern thee,' whispered the steward.

Worriedly, Thomas raised his head and looked at the steward, being sure not to look in his eyes. He had a look of fear, knowing what power the steward had over him and his family.

'Ah good, hate to see thy mother cast out into the evil of the night. Her old bones couldn't stand being away from the fire,' said the steward with a smug, sadistic smile.

The steward, pleased with his demonstration of power, walked away, quickening his pace as he neared the back door, fearful of keeping his lordship waiting too long.

'Well, that went well,' said William, looking at Thomas with a passive look of despair. He led the oxen along the gravel path to the ten-hour day of ploughing.

'What was all that about?'

'Nothing,' he realised he and he alone was responsible for the family's fortunes, or ill fortune, however God may see fit.

⁂

The deputies returned to the pillory later the next morning; the captives were motionless and filthy from the northern weather. Rotten food and the odd dead rat that had been thrown at them by the locals as they walked by. They opened the lock, and the top of the frame was removed from the pillory. Groggy and semi-unconscious from their ordeal, the two held onto the frame for fear of ripping their ear from its resting place. Their backs stiff, legs trembling, and faces cut from the odd stone thrown at them from playful children that knew of the pillory but not the reason for the punishment. Faeces and urine soaked their putrid hose and soft leather shoes. The deputy took his knife from the sheath, cutting the ear around the nail leaving a notch. The captives screamed out in pain, which woke them from their comatose state.

Free at last, they sank to their knees clutching the red, mottled perforation that was left. The corner of their ears left on the frame of the pillory for all to see and a reminder to all that passed. Blood trickled down the side of their face and escaped through the gaps between their fingers. Children on the other side of the square watched, whispered and laughed while others walked past paying no attention, more pressing duties on their minds.

'Let that be a lesson to ya's. Be gone and don't come back this way, for if I see ya', there'll be a reckoning,' said the deputy while pointing his knife at them walking by.

The deputies turned and walked away just as the vicar and his assistant came out of the chapel and helped the men to their feet. His assistant scooped water from the bucket and lifted it to the toothless one's mouth. He grabbed the pewter cup, raised it, his hands shaking, and quickly guzzled it without a breath. He lost his balance as the vicar let go of him and tended to his mate, scooping more water and offering it. Stuart tried to stand. His knees were wobbly, so he used the frame of the pillory to steady himself. He winced and held the area where his ear had been notched, but said nothing.

'God be with you, my sons, now that you have paid thy penance go in peace and let the Lord have mercy on thee.'

The coney-catchers walked out into the street. They staggered as they walked down the road. Archie lost his balance and fell in the mud; his companion helped him up and put his arm around his shoulder to support him. They walked along Belle Isle Road and then cut across the field to Bridgehouse Beck. Dropping beneath a tree to compose themselves, Archie crawled to the water's edge to wash the grime and faeces away.

Stuart wiped the congealed blood from his face and tenderly scooped water and poured it over his wound, being careful not to start the bleeding again. 'It'll take us days to get back to York.'

'We ain't going back, not yet anyway; if we can't make coin in the village, we'll make coin outside the village. Besides, there's a young bastard that needs to be taught a lesson,' said the toothless one as he removed his hose and codpiece to rinse in the beck.

'Well, what are we gonna do? We 'ave nowt. No grub, no lodgin' and besides, if that steward sees us again, we'll end up swinging from a rope.'

'Let's rest here until it gets dark, then we'll round up some grub. There's a cottage over there in that field.'

They both leant back against the tree and dozed, being careful not to sleep too heavily lest a villager happened to come walking by.

The sun was going down over the horizon when Archie woke.

'Hey wake up.' Archie kicked him on the foot, trying to rouse him. Stuart shook off his grogginess and then grimaced as he lifted his hand to touch his ear. Or what was left of it.

They consumed the rest of the chicken they had stolen from the cottage in the night.

'We'll make our way to Stanbury. Our business here is not finished. We'll come back when things have settled.' Archie stood and kicked around the ashes from the small fire.

ク

The next afternoon, Margery had emptied the waste bucket onto the mound outside where all the waste was kept, collected the water, washed the clothes, watered the animals and was now preparing to take bread and cheese to Thomas and William.

As the sun reached its highest point. She walked down the hill past the ditch where they had found Mr Hargreaves and she noticed something, a red hat. Picking it up, she turned it over and looked at the bloodied inside.

'What's this then?' She exclaimed, 'The property of Mr John Hargreaves of Moorehouse Lane, Oxenhope, I believe?' She smiled.

The hat still had a frayed hole where he had been struck. Bending down, Margery rinsed it in the ditch water and rung it out as best she could. I'll pop by the manor and give this to Agnes. *Better still, take it to the chapel on Sunday,* she thought. *No, I have a better idea!*

Margery continued on her way and arrived to find Thomas and

William tired, sweaty and overcome with the heat of the day. Only three acres had been ploughed.

'I'm glad that you are having so much fun there Thomas and teaching bad habits to thy brother. You won't be smiling so much when the seed is planted late and the harvest is poor, and we have nowt to eat.'

'Fear not mother, we were kept back entertaining business with the steward.' Only Thomas and William could see the funny side of this and snickered.

Margery showed her contempt, 'Oh yes, and what would the steward want with you two shakeragg? Unless he found something to fine ya' for. Here is thy lunch; bread, cheese 'n ale. Summer is fast approaching; you need ta beat the rains or else we're finished.'

Thomas took out a linen cloth and wiped the sweat from his brow. He and William sat at the side of the suhl and opened the cloth package containing the bread and cheese. They didn't talk much until it was all gone and washed down with a jug of ale.

'Best we keep going brother,' said Thomas, standing and turning at the waist to loosen his stiffness.

'By the way, look what I found in the ditch near home,' Margery pulled the hat out of her basket. 'John Hargreave's hat, it seems.'

CHAPTER 6

DARKEST DANGER

John stuck his head in the bucket of water and washed, trying to rid himself of the stains and memory of the previous night. He started to recall the events…

He remembered waiting for Agnes near the manor and hearing the buzz emanating from the square. It was a chilly night and thought he might climb the hill for a quick ale and warm himself by the fire, knowing that she was always late coming from the manor.

He was only going to stay for an ale or two until his two companions convinced him to go to the rat baiting in the cellar. He remembered walking down the creeping, rotten wood stairs into a large stone-walled room which was full of smoke and the stench of dead rats and loud barking dogs whipped into a frenzy by their owners. There was the acidic smell of old urine and stale ale. Oil lamps lit the centre of the room, which was cordoned off with a square of wooden planks set almost chest high. The earthen floor was blood stained at the bottom of the pit, which was home to dog fights, cock fights, and tonight's entertainment.

Men entertained themselves, yelling and arguing their point, often spraying spittle, trying to get the slightest bit of knowledge about the contestants that may positively sway their wager. The dog owners rallied support for their dog above any other. Casting wagers against owners of other dogs, excitedly.

'That little terrier, I might wager on the rat,' yelled one drunken guest.

All that heard laughed, with one elder who couldn't quite contain himself, coughing out his ale while trying to laugh and breath at the same time.

'Ayup, I seen the rats. He catches them in the cemetery; some are bigger than a house cat,' said another.

The rat catcher made his way down the wooden stairs. His hessian bag relentlessly moving with squealing, panicked rats.

He unloaded thirty rats out of the hessian bag into the pit. They scattered quickly around the pit as the crowd roared with excitement. Men filled the wooden bleachers, which climbed up the stone walls. The dogs, terrier crosses all of them, barked with excitement, pulling on the rope held by their owners. Hearing the dogs, the rats cornered themselves, climbing over one another to get to the highest point on the wall to escape, only to be knocked lower by another bigger rat. Their six-inch tails trailed behind them, their yellow teeth nipping at the rat beside and long whiskers twitching with nervousness unused to being in the light.

'Come on Billy, let's show them what you can do,' said the owner, stepping forward for his dog's turn at the mayhem.

He unroped the dog and picked him up by the scruff of the neck, holding him in mid-air on the inside of the pit. The crowd roared. The men screamed back and forth across the pit, making bets on how many rats Billy could dispense with in a minute.

'He doesn't look like much ta me, I'll wager two shillings, no more 'n fifteen rats!' yelled one patron eagerly.

'Yer, I'll take your wager and say more 'n fifteen!' said another.

The dog, seeing the rats, excitedly tried to struggle free from his owner's grasp, but he couldn't break his grip. The owner looked at the referee and waited for the signal. When the referee nodded, he dropped the dog. The timekeeper turned the minute glass as soon as the dog's paws touched the dirt. Excitedly, Billy growled and looked at the rats, his senses alert and keen. He was highly stimulated by the herbs his owner had given him and was ready to do what he had been trained to do. He hit the ground running, feverishly attacking the group of rats in the corner.

The crowd roared. Hargreaves, getting caught up in the excitement had placed his wager, declaring twenty rats as his number. His companions secretly smiled at each other, knowing that no dog could reach such a milestone. The steward's money was safe, they thought. Besides, that was the least of their worries.

The dog worked in exemplary fashion, a grip, a toss, and it was all over for the rat. Billy was very skillful and at one point bit into two rats at the same time, shaking them both in a frenzied fashion then releasing his grip and running at the corner to latch onto others. They scattered as he approached, but he was too quick and knew their habits, running close to the wall as tight as they could.

The marshal, who tried to keep some order to proceedings, called out the number of rats killed, 'One rat, two, three, four, five…' Some lay motionless, others bloodied with their entrails following them, but still alive, tried to crawl away.

'Seventeen… eighteen… nineteen… twenty… time,' said the marshal, who wrestled a dead rat from the dog's mouth and lifted Billy by the scruff of the neck, out and back to his owner. Billy wasn't finished yet and tried to fight his way out of the marshal's grip to continue.

'Ayup that rat isn't dead,' said another man who had wagered on nineteen.

The marshal stepped in. 'Right, local rats, local rules. If t' rat manages to get to the outside of the pit in a minute, then he is considered still alive, and the count will be nineteen.' The timekeeper turned over the minute glass as the referee marked a large circle with a stick on the inside circumference of the pit.

Excited, the crowd yelled at the rat, some wishing it ill health and good riddance, and others wishing it a healthy recovery.

'Ayup, it's movin', cum on, get crackin',' said one man.

The rat suffered from a lack of blood, and its two back legs were shattered. It rose up on its front paws, face smashed, and blood was oozing from its mouth and an eye socket that was missing an eye. It continued to move, and the crowd cheered as more wagers were placed on the result. The rat looked behind and tried to sniff its back legs, numbed by the crushed nerves. It pushed up on its front paws again and some of the crowd cheered. Others started to insult the owner of Billy, who they said did not do enough to kill the rat. The rat took one more step and then keeled over in exhaustion.

'TWENTY!' yelled the referee. John looked up at his companions and was shocked. 'I WON, TWENTY RATS!' He laughed ecstatically. 'I WON! I WON!'

The two men looked at each other angrily and tried to come to terms with what had eventuated as they had given him odds.

'Grand Billy, well done, lad,' the owner said, wiping the blood and left-over entrails from his chin.

He placed Billy on the floor and poured water from a bowl into his hand and continued to wash his face, being sure to allow Billy his fill to feed his thirst.

'Twenty rats killed in a minute, who'd have thought?' said one of John's companions while giving him the steward's shillings.

John held out his hand and smiled, then placed the coins in the leather purse which hung from his belt.

'Come on rounds on me!'

The steward would not be happy, knowing that they had lost his money. But that dog, how were they to know? It wasn't until later that they heard the dog had a reputation in other parts of Keighley.

'Ta, kind sirs, pleasure is mine.' John gestured for them to follow him up the stairs for a celebratory ale.

The drinks were on him; he went upstairs with his new companions. They showed him much kindness and so did the barmaid, ensuring their jacks were kept full. She knew the drill.

He didn't notice the steward on the far side of the tavern and the shrewd nod he gave to the strangers through the crowd when their eyes met his. One of them frowned with disappointment and shook his head slightly. The steward wasn't amused.

The following evening, sitting at home in Stanbury, the steward started to think about the events of the previous night. He was angry his companions had lost his wager; he didn't like common folk winning at the rat baiting that he secretly organised to coincide with each manor court. On a good night, he could win money from the locals, who had managed to scrounge for the payne, fines and dues. Without money for the payne, fines and dues, they would have to pay more the next time, some shillings for the lord and some for him. He always stayed one step ahead, knowing that if the lord's coffers were low and he lost his temper, he would have to pay it out of his own purse.

It was quite a lucrative setup. He paid a shilling to the rat catcher, a shilling to the dog owner and a portion of the winnings to his recently acquired partners. That, coupled with his skimming of the fines and dues paid, provided a lucrative income on top of the stipend which his lordship paid him to tend to manor business. That night, he thought, was supposed to be unique. He had arranged for a dog to come up from Bradford after seeing him in action down there a few weeks past. He had never seen a dog so ferocious, so cunning and quick. He lost some money on him in Bradford but expected to get it all back, and more, that evening.

The evening was even better than expected, having charmed his way into a card game with a couple of out-of-town coney-catchers. He had watched them take coin from several locals before he approached the table. He felt contempt for any outsiders that tried to cash in. These two were obviously from out of the parish, likely doing their regular rounds through the local villages. It was apparent that they were good at it for the two of them still had both their ears. They allowed him to win the first three hands, one of them raising the bet each time then bowing out to let his friend lay down cards, which were always just good enough to win the hand. They were clever enough to let him win a hand occasionally, to keep his interest, but slowly gained more and more of his purse. That was, until the watchman rang the bell for a count of eight.

CHAPTER 7
WAY OF A WOMAN

After giving Thomas and William their lunch, Margery started walking back home. She continued across the ploughed fields to Sun Street, past the broken drywall, up the hill she went where it turned into Marsh Lane. It was tough going in the heat of the day; the sun starting to get to its highest point. She finally reached the top of the hill and started down the other side. Down she went, past more cottages. She asked one of the women tending to the salting of some fish where the Hargreaves lived.

She pointed, 'Hargreaves cottage, across yonder field to Moorhouse Lane, just up the hill.'

Margery walked across the field and down the hill; and noticed the smoke coming out of the chimney. The chickens scattered and squawked as she approached.

'Ayup, are you there, Mrs Hargreaves?' she said, walking up to the door of the stone walled cottage.

'I am, 'n who might you be? I haven't seen thee in these parts before, but I've seen you at the market in Haworth.'

'Aye, and I've seen you there and thy lovely daughter.'

'What brings you down the hill?' asked Mrs Hargreaves as she continued to push the plunger in and out of the butter churner.

'This hat, I found it in the field in our ditch, thought it might be your husband's,' she said, showing it to John's wife.

'Aye it's his. You must be Mrs Rushworth, you tended ta John the night before last. You better come inside. Do you want a brew?'

'That would be fine,' said Margery. 'That walk has made me a bit parched.'

'John won't be home for ages. He's ploughing a field for the lord's grace,' said Mrs Hargreaves as she poured more ale into Margery's jack.

'Well, that's just it, I didn't come ta see John, I came ta see you,' Margery said, blushing.

Mrs Hargreaves laughed a deep belly laugh, leaning back, raising her head to the rafters, then back at Margery. 'My goodness, here to see me, what in God's name for?'

Margery smiled cunningly. 'Well, when your John were convalescing at our hearth, he mentioned your daughter Agnes who worked at the manor. Our Thomas needs a grand woman to come home to, and I was thinking…'

There's no way on earth my husband will allow Agnes to marry outside the faith. 'Our Agnes? Mmm, not sure if me husband will allow it.'

Margery took another sip of ale. 'I seen her at the market with thee on many occasion, seems like a grand lass.'

'Aye she is, we're proud of her and the woman she's become. Why her though? There's plenty of other lasses in the village.'

'Aye, there is, but widows or spoiled the lot of 'em.

'You being new to the Parish, I thought it might make a good match.'

'I'll have to speak to me husband when he gets back from the fields. Agnes' wage from the manor comes in right handy, I will speak to my husband.' *I'll not speak to him because I know what the answer will be.*

She dropped her head with the disappointment; however, the interest of a matchmaker was exciting.

'Me son Thomas is a tenant at Hall Green, but a grand lad,' claimed Margery proudly. Margery spoke convincingly, 'Not many good lads around here, most like the drink and whores at the taverns. Besides, do you want thy daughter to be a spinster her whole life?'

Worriedly, Mrs Hargreaves paused before answering, 'No course not, but this is all so sudden.' *Heavens above she is a pushy woman!*

'She would have a grand life with my Thomas, 'n God willing a baby or three. Right you are then. Let's talk again at Saint Michael and All Angels on Sunday, after prayers,' stated Margery with the overconfidence and pushiness that she was renowned for.

'Yes, let's do that Mrs Rushworth.' *There's no chance of that 'cause we won't be there! Poor Agnes, the first suitor that comes calling and I must turn them away. What is to become or our Agnes?*

Mrs Hargreaves thought back to the time when she and John had first noticed each other in church. He was a handsome man, and his father was a freeman holding his own land. They were very comfortable for a long while until it all started. Most had pledged their oath to Queen Bess, but John and his father refused to. They said their prayers in secret and held Communion under the cover of darkness; a Jesuit priest coming to their cottage in the middle of the night. They stopped going to church, and paid the penalty, losing much of what they owned to the manor court because of shillings that they had to forfeit each week.

The Hargreaves had been hoping for more religious tolerance when James came to the throne. Things got worse, and they were chastised in the village. A short time later, they left in fear of retribution, disappeared, gave up everything they had except the ox and a few trinkets.

Labour was in short supply because of the 'Black Death', so it didn't take long for John to get the lord's favour and buy a small patch of land on the outskirts of Haworth.

'I'll not promise anything, but should John wish it, you can call again,' said Mrs Hargreaves, worrying about the conversation they were having without her husband present.

It was getting late, and Margery realised that she still had to walk up the hill home, 'Goodness me, the sun is getting low in the sky and I haven't prepared the supper for me boys or got the cow in. Best I nip on quickly like.'

Mrs Hargreaves suddenly came out of deep thought, 'I need to get a move on my John will surely know somethin's amiss if things aren't orderly 'n well when he gets home. Go on, love, be off with ya' before we both have ta line up for the ducking stool.'

Margery took the last swig of the ale and handed the jack back to Mrs Hargreaves. 'Right, I will see thee Sunday then.'

Margery left and quickened her pace to beat the night watchman's bell.

John arrived home in the light of the moon. She heard him and she felt ashamed of all that had gone on in his absence. He walked in through the door, the hinges creaked, exhausted from the day's labour in the lord's field. He felt for his hat but realised he had lost it. John walked to the bench silently, almost staggering from the ten-hour overexertion. He lifted the bucket and poured water into the large wooden bowl, sticking his head in it for what seemed like an eternity. Only when he couldn't hold his breath any longer did he lift his head and release the ache in his lungs. He gasped for air and splashed his face two more times, running his hands through his sweaty dark hair. He took off his wet shirt, exposing his wiry but muscular chest and continued to wash under his armpits.

He removed his codpiece and his soiled hose, his wife picking them up in an instant and folded them ready for the next day.

Mrs Hargreaves held a linen towel silently while he splashed water under his arms and between his legs, making sure he washed away the sweat. He dried them properly to keep away the chafe. His wife gave him a clean undershirt to put on. It dangled almost to his knees, but it was fresh with the smells of a springtime day and it pleased him. He sat on his stool near the hearth, smoked from his clay pipe, and thought about the events of the day. He wasn't the only one doing the lord's bidding, and he enjoyed the comradery with the other men. There was Richard Bins, Anthony Pigshells and Robert Deane, all tenanted to the lord except for him. He enjoyed the banter; it wasn't often that there was time for laughter during the day, especially at the lord's pleasure.

Shall I tell him? Nooo best left for another time. Margery was silent, not knowing how to breach the news with her husband. She stirred the pottage in the cauldron and brought him ale to help him clear the dust from his throat.

'You are quiet wife, have you got something to say ta me?' he said in a relaxed tone.

'No husband, hold on, when you've had thy fill of ale then we will chat,' she said, trying not to give too much away about her earlier meeting with Margery Rushworth.

Mrs Hargreaves handed him the bowl. He devoured the contents and a second helping, gulping ale to wash it down. He paused and stilled himself.

'Tell us wife, does our chat have anything ta do with me hat sitting there on the table?'

John asked, mesmerised by the fire.

Mrs Hargreaves realised Margery had left the hat, so she walked over and hung it on the nail near the door.

'So, it seems you had the pleasure of a visit from Mrs Rushworth today,' said John as he took a puff of his pipe.

'And what did you discuss wife?'

'Nothing except the time a' day husband.'

'Seems a long walk just ta talk about the time a' day.'

Mrs Hargreaves looked at John curiously. 'We had a chat while I was churning the butter.' His wife stood to stoke the fire and stir the pottage because hadn't eaten yet.

She's holding something back, I can feel it. John was fixated on her discussion with Margery and waited patiently for her to provide more detail of their conversation.

'Oh husband, what conversations women folk have while churning butter would you be interested in?' she replied, wanting to keep women's business to the women and knowing that now was not the time to complicate things by saying too much.

'Come now, don't let the goings on of the day worry you and what of the ploughing?' she asked, changing the subject while pouring him more ale.

'One field is finished, I must go back tomorra' with Richard, Anthony and Robert Deane, to finish t'other.'

He sat back against the wall, exhausted, re-filling his clay pipe. He knew not to push too hard, for the wife's secrets always made their way to his ears at some point, either by her mouth or by others. He was well known in the village and knew that if it were anything serious, she would confide in him sooner.

Some things are best left unsaid, especially when it's women's business. Best kept for another day, he thought to himself.

He took a puff of his pipe, watching the embers in the bowl of it redden, then he slowly blew out, watching the smoke mingle with the smoke from the fire and drift toward the rafters.

CHAPTER 8

WAY OF A WOMAN

Margery had gotten used to hearing services in English and not Latin. She could understand what the minister was saying, and it wasn't just the scriptures. She especially liked sermons with tid bits of notices and news, the king's news. Now, the congregation was urged to read the Bible, but most of them were illiterate, so relied on the vicar to inform them of God's will.

From the pulpit the vicar sermonised the Homily on Marriage.

'The woman is a weak creature not endowed with the like strength and constancy of mind as men. Therefore, they be the sooner disquieted and they be the more prone to weak affections and dispositions of the mind more than men be.'

Margery liked coming to the Saint Michael and All Angels. She thought it was a magnificent building and remembered coming here as a child when all was in Latin and the Catholic Holy Communion was the order of the day. It was only thirty paces from door to alter; the thick stone walls kept it relatively cool inside on the hottest of summer days. The large circular patterns adorning the walls displaying bible scenes, saints' apostles, angels and Christ, all painted in reds, ochres, yellows. The barrel-vaulted ceiling rising to the heavens from the plain, wooden pews below. The chapel entrance was embellished with ornate stone carving. The large wooden cross was crowned by a small opening in the wall, which held the oil lamp. shedding its dim light over the altar.

Margery heard the door vibrate with the wind. She looked around, paused, then faced the front, listening to the end of the lengthy sermon from the vicar.

'The goodman or master of the family is a person in whom resteth the private and proper government of the whole household: and he comes to it not by election… but by the ordinance of God, settled even in the course of nature.'

And he paused.

'—The goodwife of the house is a person which yieldeth help and assistance in government to the master of the family. For he is, as it were, the prince and chief ruler; she is the associate.'

She wondered why Mrs Hargreaves, John and Agnes were absent from church. These were not times to be absent and surely, they would face the two-shilling fine, she thought.

The vicar, having finished his sermon called upon his congregation to remain seated. Several wives and daughters remained seated, looking at their husbands and fathers with contempt as they quickly rose to make a quick exit. The men received particular attention from the warden who was responsible for order in the church.

The vicar repeated, 'Dearest folk, please remain seated. I have news from London, a bill has been passed by Parliament outlawing Catholicism. Jesuit priests are being rounded up and imprisoned. Any found harbouring them will feel the full brunt of the law.'

The congregation was shocked, as King James had promised a more religious tolerance. Some started to whimper, others sat there motionless.

The vicar went on, 'God save the King.'

'God save the King! God save the King!' the congregation repeated together, following the vicar's lead.

They then recited the Lord's Prayer.

'Wee Father whoa art in heaven, hallowed be thy name. Thy kingdom come thy will be done, on earth as it is in heaven. Give us this day daily bread; 'n forgive our trespasses, as we forgive them who trespass against us; lead us not into temptation, but deliver wee from evil.'

The congregation stood and started filing out of the pews towards the door at the back of the church. Margery was still looking for the Hargreaves as she strolled through the big oak door out into the day.

She was followed by William and Thomas. 'What's wrong mother? You look distracted?' asked William with a concerned look on his face.

'I'm fine son, just thankin' God for the day.' Sunday was always a good day, she thought, a rest from the routine work and chores. She also felt a sadness for the minority of recusant Catholics that lived in the village and the Keighley surrounds.

'William, mother is just feeling full of the sermon,' said Thomas, smiling, and thinking about the upcoming 'ball' and ale.

'William don't show disrespect ta the Lord 'n saviour, less you want ta fetch damnation on the family,' said Margery, looking back and frowning in contempt. *We'll see how smart you are when I reveal my little secret my son.*

CHAPTER 9

RAVAGED VISIONS

William escorted Margery toward home while Thomas met with the other village men in preparation for 'ball' against East'ards. Ball was always a fiery affair and Thomas enjoyed the comradery that it generated. Every man in Haworth that could walk was expected to participate, and the game would be celebrated and discussed for weeks afterwards.

Two upright poles were placed in the paddock just east of Moorhouse Lane and another set was placed just west of Haworth Road, about one and a half miles away. The two groups of men numbered about three hundred, but nobody knew for sure.

The game would start on the eastern side of Bridgehouse Beck, where the ball would be thrown into the crowd of men vying for a touch. The ball, a leather-bound sheep's bladder, was thrown into the melee. Many reached for it and it bounced away westerly on the sea of grasping hands. It disappeared below the crush only to resurface after a fiery encounter below.

One came up throwing the ball west, another clutching his broken nose. Movement of the ball was stalled by many a hand, then it disappeared again. The crowd moved into the Bridgehouse Beck waters, but they were halted on the bank by a huge oak tree. One of the players of the East'ards climbed the tree on the other side and perched on a limb. The ball was thrown up to him and two from the West'ards climbed up after him, trying to free the ball from his clasp. The three of them fell from the tree onto the waiting crowd below. Two of them got up again to continue, but the third who fell didn't move. The crowd, a moving, clutching sea of bodies moving over him indiscriminately kicking and pushing, not sparing their weight or number.

As the melee continued slowly westward, four men were left behind, one clutching his dislocated shoulder. The other was bleeding profusely from a cut in his head and the other two laid quiet and still curled in an awkward position on the damp ground.

At the centre of the crowd, two men tussled for possession of the ball, three others grabbed at their tunics trying to pull them away. Four of the East'ards pushed, and gradually the ball moved further until it popped up at the top of the crowd. All in proximity tried to hit it and for a time it did move easterly. It sunk into the sea of bodies once again, one man holding it with eight of his folk pushing in front.

Two West'ards men, seeing what they were doing, managed to grab the ball carrier's arm, but as the crowd surged forward, his arm was caught and angled backwards the opposite way of movement. There was an almighty scream from him as his arm was caught. The West'ards men still had hold of it until they heard the 'pop' and consequent scream, the bone coming from its socket. He dropped the ball and clung to his shoulder, and the ball hung in limbo for a while, possessed by neither team but supported by the numerous bodies.

That was, until Thomas happened on it. He bent his head down and cradled the ball. Some were pulling his doublet eastward, others pulling him westward. His tunic ripped, but he held onto the ball. One of the East'ards jumped up and over two men and latched onto his hair. He dropped the ball and wrestled his hair from the man's grasp. The ball continued to move in a westerly direction through valley and vale, over dry-stone walls, through a blackberry bramble and at one point, through a vegetable garden. The wife and mother screamed blue murder from inside the cottage, fearful of going outside.

It wasn't until sunset when the ball had finally been maneuvered through the poles just east of Moorhouse Lane and the East'ards celebrated their victory with cheers of celebration. They shook hands with those closest to them. Tired and tattered, they made their way home for a celebratory ale at their favourite alehouse. Some limped, others had minor cuts and abrasions from the day's play.

Thomas made his way home, ripped tunic, scratched, bruised, sore and sorry for himself that they had lost the day.

⁂

Earlier, while Thomas was off playing 'ball', William escorted Margery home. As they approached, Margery continued to walk down the hill, past the cottage. 'Where are you going mother? Have you lost your mind?'

'William be silent, I have business to attend to. Now nip on home 'n stoke the fire,' she said as she made her way down the hill.

Down she went, past more cottages, across the field and there it was, the Hargreaves stone cottage. There was smoke coming from the chimney and the cattle door was open. There was no sign of John in the field, but she remembered it was Sunday as she noticed Mrs Hargreaves walk past the door.

She walked up to the cottage timidly, not wanting to surprise and scare her out of her wits. 'Ayup, Mrs Hargreaves are you there?' she called out. There was no answer. 'Mrs Hargreaves? It's me, Margery Rushworth, I missed you at church. I thought I'd come by,' she yelled while sticking her head in the door.

Suddenly, Mrs Hargreaves just appeared. 'Why don't you just leave us alone?' she exclaimed angrily.

Margery was shocked by the outburst. 'Oh, I am so sorry Mrs Hargreaves, I missed you at church and wondered if something were wrong.'

Disappointedly, Margery turned away. 'I'm sorry ta have disturbed you, so I'll be on my way. Good day ta thee Mrs Hargreaves.'

As she turned and started walking back through the field, she heard a soft whimpering coming from the cottage. She turned and went back, stuck her head once again in the cattle door. Allowing time for her eyes to adjust, she saw Mrs Hargreaves seated at a stool, face in hands sobbing. She undid the latch and went in.

Margery walked up to Mrs Hargreaves and put her hand on her shoulder. 'There, there pet, what's troubling you ta make you so sad on this beautiful day? Has t' husband beaten you? Av you lost a calf. Pray Lord, tell me!'

Looking up at Margery through tears, 'I'm so sorry for bein' rude to you, I don't know what ta do,' she broke down again, sobbing into her hands.

'There, there pet. Whatever it is, we can help,' claimed Margery in a soft, empathetic tone.

Mrs Hargreaves stopped sobbing and wiped her eyes with her apron. Then she peered up and explained why they hadn't been at church. 'Mrs Rushworth, I was so pleased when we last spoke, but I must tell you a secret but you must swear not to tell a soul. We are recusant Catholics.' She cupped her face in her hands and began to sob once again.

'There, there, pet.' Putting her hand on Mrs Hargreaves shoulder, she reassured her. 'I have no ill feelings towards you or yours, but sadly, I feel the union between our families can't go ahead. We have no wish to suffer the ire of the king or his church.'

Mrs Hargreaves sobbed again. 'Please, please help us. I fear for my daughter Agnes.'

'Shuush now pet, no more tears, of course I'll help! Don't you worry yerself now. Remember, we were all of the faith at one time. It is what it is.'

Mrs Hargreaves could have never dreamed that a poor peasant woman from the moors would have such a profound effect on the future of her family.

'Come now, let me get you a brew,' Margery walked over to the wooden barrel and poured, handing the leather jack to Mrs Hargreaves.

'John is a stubborn man like his father before him and has refused to take the oath of allegiance to the English church these past two years.'

She then recounted how difficult it had been in their previous parish and how John gave up his land to leave and take up residence where they were not known. She told of how careful they had been to leave in the darkness of the night, without even as much as a goodbye to their family and friends.

Worriedly, Margery whispered, 'You must conform or else receive the penalties and forfeitures, you could lose your land. Have you not heard about the magistrate in York who hanged a priest and another Catholic for no other offence other than their beliefs and secret prayers?'

Mrs Hargreaves gazed up at her. 'We were in expectation that the laws would be more tolerant under King James, but since they tried to blow up Parliament, the laws have been set against us. So much so that we live in constant fear for our own Agnes and the repercussions that would be directed at her if his lordship were to find out.'

'Mrs Hargreaves, at the church the vicar told us of the king's solemn decree. You have forty days to hear the divine service or risk conviction and lose thy land or worse. If you go to the church and hear the divine service, all is saved,' said Margery in a sympathetic tone.

'That decision is not mine, but my husband's,' claimed Mrs Hargreaves looking at her in despair.

'You must tell him, convince him for Agnes' sake, for his and for your own. If not, then you must register with the justice of the peace and thou cannot travel out. You will be fined each Sunday service. Then… they will come looking for ya' and if they catch you, you'll be imprisoned. You'll lose yer land and who knows what else.'

Mrs Hargreaves broke down again whimpering, 'I know not what to do.'

At that point, the door opened and John walked in, surprised to see that his wife had company and was distraught.

He was bent over in pain and groaned. 'What's going on here, then?' he grumbled, assuming their secret had been exposed.

Moaning, he held his forearm up against his chest, grimacing in pain.

'Are you okay Mr Hargreaves? Have you done harm to yourself?' Margery asked.

Mrs Hargreaves, with puffy, red eyes, wiped the tears and stood to tend to her husband. 'What's wrong husband? You look like you're in pain.'

He was bent over, his arm dangling loosely toward the floor.

'Can I help you?' Margery asked, waiting for reassurance from the couple.

She had seen this before. His arm looked as if it had come loose from the shoulder. Through his shirt, she could see a lump, a bone protruding from his upper arm.

The two women helped him over to the wooden form where they carefully sat him down. Mrs Rushworth lightly held his arm. 'Hold him Mrs.' She directed Mrs Hargreaves to hold him around the chest.

She then put her foot on his ribs under his arm and held tightly. She started to straighten her knee, and slowly pulled. He groaned, she pulled harder, he groaned louder, and then with one last effort she pulled with all her might. They all heard a clunk. Mr Hargreaves frowned face turned instantly into one of relief; he stood clutching his shoulder, amazed by the absence of pain.

Mr Hargreaves, receiving a mug of ale from his wife, went on to explain how when playing ball, the crowd had surged forward, and his arm had been wrestled behind him. It was then that his disfigurement had occurred. He explained how he had dropped the ball, but it was too late, the damage had been done.

'Mrs Rushworth, it is the second time in as many weeks that you have come to my aid and I don't know how to repay you,' he said, rubbing his shoulder.

Margery walked toward the door, peered at Mrs Hargreaves, not letting on, but silently encouraging her to discuss with her husband what they had talked about. He noticed their eyes connect and turned to look at his wife. *What are these two up to?* he asked himself.

'I best be going, leave you two to your business, tarreur then,' she said while lifting the latch and closing the cattle door behind her.

'Husband, we must talk. There's trouble brewing in the village. We have forty days ta visit divine service or else risk retribution from the justice. We will lose the land and Agnes will lose her duties at the manor. We'll be done for husband.'

'Not if we leave for London Town,' replied John, still rubbing his shoulder. 'We could disappear again.'

'Lose all that we've worked for again?' asked his wife sadly. 'Then there's the sickness about in London. What of poor Agnes? She doesn't deserve a life like this.'

'Margaret! You know my thought on the subject!'

He only called her Margaret when he was angry. Mrs Hargreaves knew not to push him too far.

She gazed at him sadly. *There's nothing I can do. We're done for.*

Seeing her melancholy, he knew he had to do something. 'Let us sleep on it wife, my heart is saddened 'n my mind is muddled,' he said tiredly, slowly standing.

He walked to his chair and sat, took out his clay pipe while looking to the hearth.

She watched him gazing through the flames in deep thought.

Later that night she heard and felt him climb into bed, much later than usual, with the rustle of the straw mattress. She could tell that he wasn't sleeping. He didn't move, but she knew his eyes were open, staring into the darkness.

It was a long night, and she didn't sleep much either; Marg put another log on the fire to warm the room. She looked over at Agnes; her long dark hair glistened from the glow of the fire.

Mrs Hargreaves thought about when her parents had arranged her marriage to John. They had only met weeks before the wedding, and now it had been 25 years. Neither of them would say it was marital bliss, but he was a good man and she had heard stories of worse.

Agnes stirred as the fire got warmer and brighter. She would have to wake soon to dress and make her way to the manor before the cock crowed. She could have stayed there with the other servants but chose to stay at home, helping her mother when she could.

Agnes always started early enough to tend the fire under the three-legged pot where the lord's porridge simmered; and collected the eggs from the chicken coup before the cook and the three others arrived from their servant's quarters upstairs.

Agnes and the other kitchen maids feared not only the chastisement from the cook but also the birch whip, which he kept in the corner as a continual reminder of the need for humbleness and hard work. It had taken her a while to get used to the efficiency of the kitchen but was now an expert at simmering the sauces, roasting on the spit and ensuring there were enough utensils and clean pots.

John dressed and moved toward the hearth to warm himself. His shoulder hurt, but there was ploughing to be done.

'Did you sleep well husband?' asked his wife as she handed him a bowl of oats.

'I think you know the answer to that question, wife,' as he remembered their discussion from the previous evening.

Well, I may as well tell him. 'There is one other thing I need to discuss with you husband. Mrs Rushworth has spoken of a union, her son Thomas and our Agnes.' She felt guilty about not mentioning it earlier and got ready for the angry rhetoric that she thought would come.

John paused, but the scathing words that Mrs Hargreaves expected didn't eventuate.

He took a deep breath and blew out in frustration. 'So wife, I am to lose my God and now our daughter?' he whispered sadly.

Mrs Hargreaves whispered to keep the news from Agnes who was sleeping nearby. 'So, you have decided then?'

'Best to do so than risk the justice's rack and burning tongs. We cannot continually hide our thoughts and feelings, for Agnes' sake. She will be wanting to make her own way in the world soon and we shouldn't make this journey harder for her than it needs to be.'

'They seem like a good family; you best arrange to meet with Mrs

Rushworth again wife. It is time Agnes became a woman. Sunday.' He said, then abruptly finished the last spoonful of oats, last gulp of ale and left, walking out the door into the darkness.

Agnes had heard all this while lying there, pretending to be asleep. She raised herself on her forearms with a quizzical look.

'Mother,' she whispered. 'Why didn't you tell me?'

She sat up, her hair cascading over the side of her face. Realising her father had gone, she knew there was no reason to whisper.

'This is business for your father, not for you daughter,' her mother said sternly as she took John's bowl and cup to the wash bucket in the kitchen.

'I don't want to get married; I want to stay here with you,' she said while placing her linen smock over her head, followed by the sleeveless kirtle. She put on her partlet, which covered her arms and upper torso, tied back her hair and finished off the ensemble with a wimple that she tightened on her head.

Agnes was a pure country beauty; she had large, confident green eyes crowned with dark, thickish eyebrows, high cheekbones and long eyelashes. Her nose was straight with a cute button tip, giving her an angelic look. Her lips were naturally red and plump, and her smile warmed the hearts of whoever spoke to her. Her face was framed by wisps of dark hair that had escaped from her wimple. Her skin was pale from working such long hours in the kitchen at the manor, but there was an adventurous, outgoing and strong-willed air about her.

'Mother, do I not have a say in the matter at all? What if he's a brute that beats me?' she asked alarmingly, 'Or even worse, sends me to the ducking stool to be dunked like a washed linen shirt.'

'No, you don't have a say in it. The decision is your fathers to make,' she said with a wise sentiment.

'Best you tend to the goings and comings of the household with care girl,' she said, smiling, knowing that by all accounts from the people she had approached on the subject, the family were upstanding citizens of the parish.

'Mother, who is he?'

'Thomas Rushworth of Hall Green, tenant to Lord Birkhead.'

'Tenant to Lord Birkhead, Mother, he's a peasant and not of the faith!'

'Yes well, at present beggars can't be choosers.'

'MOTHER I WON'T DO IT!'

'Lower your voice Agnes, you will do what your father asks and that is that. He knows the family and I have asked about him in the village. The family is well respected. If you're lucky, you'll have a fine man like your father and have many strong young 'uns to help you sow and harvest the fields. If not, at least you'll have a roof over your head and food in your stomach after we're gone.'

⁂

Further up the hill, Margery walked through the half-ploughed field. She could see William chopping wood in the distance. She wondered how to approach the subject of Agnes with Thomas. Margery had heard that she was a pleasant child, but was she for him? Two-thirds of the women in the village were either unfit or widows, but Agnes was young, healthy and unspoilt. The fact they were Recusant Catholics was an issue, but that was not the fault of Agnes and besides, they were freeholders. *Best to wait before telling him anything*, she thought.

When Thomas got back, Margery was impatiently waiting for him. 'My goodness Thomas, where have you been? I've been worried sick,' said Margery.

William piped in, 'He's been playin' ball mother and they lost.'

'Quiet William,' said Thomas in an angry and disgruntled tone.

'And look at thy tunic ripped, take it off straight away 'n I'll mend it for the morning,' Margery took hold of her mending box she kept on the shelf.

⁂

Sunday came around quickly. Thomas, William and Margery woke early to the bell of Saint Michael of All Angels dressed in their Sunday best, and walked the half mile to the church. It was a glorious morning and summer was painting her best day.

They walked into the chapel and through the great oak door, taking a pew mid- way down the aisle. Margery looked for the Hargreaves, but they were absent again. She had hoped that they would venture up the hill last week, but she was disappointed not to see them. It wouldn't be long before the wardens made a note of their absences after checking attendance against the manor court roll.

The vicar, newly appointed by the church council, had been commissioned to preach and instruct the people of Keighley in the true doctrine of the Gospel of Christ. Yet he was unprepared and theologically illiterate; his saving grace was the people of Haworth didn't know that and looked to him for guidance in the new ways of the church.

The parishioners were responding well and repeating each line of the prayer, after the vicar. When the door opened again; John, Mrs Hargreaves and Agnes walked in. Everybody in the church turned then whispered to the person sitting beside them.

Margery turned, smiled and turned back around. Thank *goodness for that, she convinced him.*

Thomas recognised John, his gaze lingered briefly looking at the young woman. *That must be his daughter Agnes, a stranger to Sunday service*, he thought.

With a stubborn but apologetic look on his face, John took off his hat and directed his family to one of the rows in the back of the church. He noticed Margery, William, and Thomas sitting in the pew a few rows down from them.

The vicar recited from the Book of Common Prayer,

'Almighty God, our heavenly Father, who settest the solitary in families: We commend to thy continual care the homes in which thy people dwell. Put far from them, we beseech thee, every root of

bitterness, the desire of vainglory, and the pride of life. Fill them with faith, virtue, knowledge, temperance, patience, godliness. Knit together in constant affection those who, in holy wedlock, have been made one flesh. Turn the hearts of the parents to the children, and the hearts of the children to the parents; and so, enkindle fervent charity among us all, that we may evermore be kindly affectioned one to another; through Jesus Christ our Lord. Amen.'

The congregation repeated *'Amen.'*

John stood up. 'Begging your pardon, vicar.'

'Yes, my son, what is it?'

'I have something to say…'

The congregation turned and looked at John, whispering excitedly to the person closest to them.

The vicar, hearing this raised his voice, 'Please, please, this is the house of the Lord, please show patience and mercy to this family.'

He had spoken to John previously and explained to him what was required. John, unable to read or write, practiced what was meant to be said by reciting the words after the vicar. They sat on a bench outside the church and practiced until John could recite it word for word.

The vicar knew what was going to transpire. He hushed the crowd, 'People of Haworth please be silent so that we can hear this man speak. PLEASE, PLEASE, please be quiet.'

This was the cue for the two wardens, members of the church council, to stand and hush the crowd as they walked down the aisle. The congregation went silent in expectation.

John, still standing, was joined by his wife and Agnes, who, embarrassed, looked toward the vicar pretending that there was nobody else in the room. Agnes could feel all eyes on her and briefly looked up to see Thomas glance at her with a nod of support; she looked down again quickly, not wanting their eyes to meet.

'I, Johnathon Hargreaves…' John stopped and looked at the vicar and he smiled back with a nod of encouragement to continue.

'Do humbly confess and acknowledge, that I have grievously offended God in condemning his majesty's Godly and lawful government and authority, by being absent from church and from hearing divine service, contrary to the Godly laws and statutes of this realm…' John stopped again.

The vicar mouthed the words which helped him remember. 'I am heartily sorry for the same and do acknowledge and testify in my conscience, that the bishop or see of Rome has not, nor ought to have, any power or authority over his majesty, or within any of his majesty's realms or dominions and I do promise and protest, without any dissimulation, or any colour or means of any dispensation, that from henceforth I will from time to time obey and perform his majesty's laws and statutes, in repairing to the church, and hearing divine service, and do my utmost endeavour to maintain and defend the same.' John, Agnes and Mrs Hargreaves took their seats, looking timid and also relieved.

The church was silent. 'Thank you, Mr Hargreaves,' said the vicar. 'We will look forward to your company each week for the service; now let us pray.'

'O God our King, by the resurrection of your Son Jesus Christ on the first day of the week, you conquered sin, put death to flight, and gave us the hope of everlasting life: Redeem all our days by this victory; forgive our sins, banish our fears, make us bold to praise you and to do your will; and steel us to wait for the consummation of your kingdom on the last great Day; through the same Jesus Christ our Lord. Amen.'

The congregation repeated, 'Amen.' As did John Hargreaves. *Forgive me, Father,* he thought to himself.

The vicar waited for the congregation to settle. 'It is with great sorrow that I inform you that the 'Black Death' has once again spread its net over London and York. Punishment prepared of the Lord, for consuming a people that have sinned against him no doubt. Dear people of Haworth stay vigilant and report any sickness to the steward and late-night travellers to the night watchman. Most importantly, repent, pray and ask our Lord and Saviour for forgiveness from your sins. God bless you all.'

The two wardens walked down the aisle, opened the large oak door just in time for the vicar to walk through to wait for the congregation outside.

The Hargreaves were the first to leave, not wasting any time, save embarrassment and condemnation from the parishioners; they walked quickly across the square and made their way to Sun Street for the walk down the hill. Mrs Hargreaves, however, took her time shuffling along, head down, deep in thought.

CHAPTER 10

THE BEGINNING'S BRIDE

William, Thomas and Margery walked out into the sun shielding their eyes; Margery looked, hoping to see the Hargreaves outside but there was no sign of them. She was disappointed but understood considering the circumstances of the morning. They walked across the square and made their way to Sun Street for the walk home, William and Thomas walking ahead. 'Mrs Rushworth… Mrs Rushworth!'

Margery looked around.

The vicar was holding up his cloth, so he didn't trip on it, running to catch up to her distraught with his overexertion.

'One of the parishioners asked me to give you this.' He bent over to catch his breath and secretively placed something in her hand.

'She said you would know who it was from.'

'Thank you, vicar,' she took whatever it was that the vicar had given her over to the shade of a tree.

He, meanwhile, still trying to catch his breath, walked awkwardly back toward the church, stopping for a moment to turn and look towards the tree where Margery was standing.

She stood there for a moment and watched Thomas and William saunter down Sun Street. She was proud of her sons and the way they had matured since the passing of their father. She opened her hand and in it was a small piece of woven cloth which she unfolded. On it was a charcoal etching, a rudimentary drawing of a man and a woman holding hands. In the middle was a setting sun, at the bottom was a cottage. She smiled and continued walking down Sun Street after the boys.

By this time William and Thomas were out of sight, Margery ambled home enjoying the peace and quiet of the moors. A contrast to the vivid green farms, the thick, pink, bushy carpet of bell heather was just starting to flower and played out its drama as far as the eye could see. She could hear the songs of the red grouse and golden plover, and the clouds climbing over the hills cast moving shadows with the breeze. Margery thought about the possible union between Thomas and the Hargreaves girl. Now that John Hargreaves had converted, the union was appropriate, right age, similar backgrounds and financial circumstances. Another positive attribute was that she had an income and having worked at the manor could run a household well, she hoped. Margery thought of Mrs Hargreaves, always working, could make her own ale, worked in the fields, mended clothes. Surely this would have rubbed off on Agnes she thought. The only question that remained was could she have children.

Margery briefly thought about the two boys she had lost to whooping cough, 'God rest their souls,' she said quietly to herself, feeling the pangs of sadness.

⁂

Arriving back at the cottage, Agnes was distraught with the idea of leaving her parents and her home. Her father was outside, and she dare not say much to him in fear. But she approached her mother. 'Mother, I don't want ta go, please,' she whispered, fearing her father may hear her objections.

Turning from the cauldron, Mrs Hargreaves reached up and placed both hands gently on Agnes' face and she responded in an empathetic tone, 'Now, you listen here lass this is not thy decision 'n besides your father has already made up his mind. There is nowt I can do about it.'

'You can convince him. Tell him we need the coin from the manor.'

'You must be joking, I'll do no such thing!'

She thought about when their union had been arranged, they respected each other. Even liked each other, but as time went on, there was a quiet love that John would never admit to. He showed his love in different ways by bringing her the odd bunch of spring flowers picked at the side of the road. A slight touch on her shoulder as he walked by while she sat on the stool milking the cow. A small piece of linen purchased on her birthday. She smiled, thinking how lucky she was and hoped that Agnes could feel a similar affection one day.

Deep down, she knew that the union between Agnes and Thomas was a good match and wanted to see her daughter married and taken care of. The idea of her left alone after they were gone made her melancholy. *What would she do?* They had no other family in the area and their previous parish was far away. Besides, who knows if their kin were still there or worse, taken ill of the sickness. *No, their life was here,* she thought to herself.

Agnes raised her voice, 'MOTHER PLEASE DON'T MAKE ME DO THIS!' Her eyes started to water.

At that point, the wooden door opened and John, ducking his head, walked in bringing dried peat for the fire which he dropped by the hearth.

'Wife best cut some salted meat for pottage this evening. Make sure there's plenty of ale and keep on thy Sunday best,' he demanded.

'There, there, daughter, it's the best for all of us. Dry thy eyes go put on your best, we are having visitors this evening,' she said, ushering Agnes away to the box where they kept their most precious things.

Mrs Hargreaves didn't look up at John but looked behind to see the state of Agnes who had her back to her. John noticed the quiet uneasiness in the room, leaving women's business to the women.

Sitting down on the stool, he took out his pipe and lit it slowly, puffing to get a good ember going. He paused and finally relented, 'What is it wife? This quiet is deathly. Is there something troubling you?' He asked in a dismissive tone, trying hard to be disinterested while re-lighting his pipe with a piece of straw.

Looking over at Agnes who still had her back to the room. 'Daughter, we have visitors tonight, so look thy best 'n hurry up, help thy mother lay clean straw 'n clean the mess.'

John walked outside and tended to the animals. He moved the ox and cow into the enclosure at the end of the cottage and shepherded the sheep in so that they were safe for the night. He topped the hay crib and filled the water tank.

Mrs Hargreaves moved position in the room, so that she could see him through the doorway, but he couldn't see her because of the contrasting light. He stood, leaning his foot on the top of the wood chopping block, elbow on knee. He was deep in thought, not showing an inkling of emotion. However, she knew this was a very sad time for him. He loved his princess more than life itself and would do anything to ensure her future.

While standing there, he thought about the loss of his two young sons to sickness, but quickly dismissed it from his mind, fearful of the pain it brought.

⁊ᚴ

Meanwhile, Thomas and William had arrived back at the cruck house; they were inquisitive about why she had lagged so far behind until Thomas looked back and noticed her talking with the vicar at the top of the hill.

They each helped themselves to a jack of ale and a piece of dark bread that Margery had baked that morning. The mastiff pups, realising they were home, came in the open door and laid at their feet.

'I felt sorry for poor young lass who had ta stand up beside her father at the chapel,' said Thomas.

Swallowing his mouthful of ale, William replied arrogantly, 'Bloody Recusant Catholics, should 'av done away with them years ago.' William echoed the general will of the people in the parish who had become quite beloved of Queen Bess and the English church she represented and fought for.

'Don't say that William, times are changing 'n we have ta change with 'em,' replied Thomas. 'We 'ave to be more tolerant.'

Margery walked in through the door, 'Ayup you two, don't get too comfortable, it might be Sunday but there's still work ta be done, animals need sorting. Besides, we have an errand ta run this night, so no ball today!'

'What were you talking to the vicar about mother?' Asked Thomas.

'Church business Thomas, just church business, nothing to worry yourself about,' replied Margery, before adding, 'Cousin Mary is coming with us this evening.'

'Mother, in God's name where are we going?' enquired Thomas, all the while William looked on quizzically awaiting an answer.

Well, I might as well tell 'im. 'You remember John Hargreaves? Well… you are going to meet Mrs Hargreaves and Agnes Hargreaves tonight.'

'What fer?'

'Well, no point in holding it back anymore. If everything goes according to plan, you are going to court her and marry her, and that's that,' said Margery.

'Mother, what have you done?' exclaimed Thomas. 'SHE'S CATHOLIC!'

'NOT ANYMORE SHE'S NOT! You'll do as yer told and that's that!'

'I have no need to get married yet,' he said in a rebellious tone.

Smiling, looking at his brother, William hesitated, then decided to comment, 'There, there, brother. Mother, he were soft on her at the church. Couldn't take his eyes off her, he couldn't.'

Punching William in the arm, Thomas became angry at his suggestion then stood up. 'Shut up William before ah give you a hiding.'

Lamenting, 'Mother, I said I just felt sorry for her having ta stand up in front of the village, that's orl.'

'Well,' said Margery, 'You'll get a chance to tell her yourself this evening. Now, go pick some spring flowers and bring them back so that I can make a posy for you to give to her.'

'MOTHER! Am I not master of the house now? How could ya' arrange all this without as much as a word?'

'When you are married and have young ones, then you can be master of the house, for now BE OFF WITH YA'!' she said, raising her voice in that way she did just before she brought out the whipping stick.

The two young men slowly walked out the door to tend to the animals for the night and to do as their mother asked. They were not fearful of the lash but fearful of the loss of dignity represented by the whipping stick, something they remembered painfully, but usually imparted by their father.

⁂

'Quickly, Agnes, help me move the table to the centre of the room near the fire,' instructed Mrs Hargreaves.

Agnes placed a clay jug of ale on the table with several wooden bowls and spoons. Mrs Hargreaves placed a wooden platter of fresh rye bread that she had baked this morning for the occasion.

Agnes had spread the new straw on the floor. She nervously stirred the pottage simmering in the cauldron under the chimney. Her face was flushed, partly because of the radiant heat from the fire and partly because of the blush when she thought back to seeing Thomas looking at her in church. She hadn't much to do with menfolk. Well, except Johnny Nutter, the baker who occasionally tried to steal a kiss in the bake room at the manor.

She was urgently brought out of her thoughts by her mother, who had a panicked voice. 'Ask your father to come in. They will be here soon, the sun is starting to set, and the moon will rise swiftly tonight.'

Agnes went outside to find her father pottering around the vegetable patch, scratching at the dirt with his hoe.

'Father, mother asked if you could come inside now.'

'Tell her I'll be in soon.' He leant the hoe against the wattle fence. 'AGNES wait, come here daughter. I know you are not happy about this, but it is for the best I assure you.'

Agnes shook her head, 'Father, I dread it!'

'With no sons of my own, when I and your mother go, the land will pass to you and then to your husband. Thomas Rushworth may not be a freeman, but he knows the way of the land and how to work it. Furthermore, having a husband not of the faith will protect you.'

She still wasn't convinced. 'I do this for you father and no other.' She turned and walked toward the door of the cottage.

John looked down at the ground, hoping he was doing the right thing. He started to walk toward the lightness emanating from the open door. As he did, he heard the dogs bark and the voices of people near.

They had walked up the hill along Marsh Lane. 'Mr Hargreaves, it is Mrs Rushworth and family coming,' she called out, so as not to alarm him.

Thomas held the torch aloft so that John could see their faces.

'Mother Rushworth,' he paused, 'Thomas,' he walked up to him and shook his hand. 'A pleasure to see you again. Maybe I can repay your hospitality and kindness. Please come in,' he said, as he directed them toward the cottage door.

Mrs Hargreaves responded to her husband's greetings and stood at the door smiling. 'Hello Mrs Rushworth and a hearty welcome to you and your family; please come in, let us wet your thirst and fill your tummy.'

John waited. As they approached, he ushered them into the cottage, putting his hand against the door to provide a wider entrance. 'The wife has added meat to pottage just for you, Agnes brought it home from the manor yesterday.' They each stepped through the door, ducking as they went into the cottage that was lit by the fire at the chimney and impromptu oil burners that had been placed in positions of advantageous illumination. The cottage was warm and inviting and more significant than their cruck house.

A layered stone and mud structure with a thatch roof, the chimney was the focal point of discussion, allowing the smoke from the fire to escape. The hay crib was at the end of the cottage but cordoned off by a small wall; the ox, three lambs and a cow helped themselves to the hay on offer. A large half barrel, filled with water, was close by for the animals to drink and often for John to dunk his head in after too many ales. The chickens and the rooster were in for the night and spent their time scratching at the fresh straw on the floor for any maggots that they were lucky enough to find. In the centre of the room was the bed and at its foot the dowry chest, an exceptionally large one full of all manner of collectables to make married life more comfortable.

Agnes and her mother were very proud of the things contained in the chest; they had been collecting and making since she was a little girl, even before she knew its purpose.

The inner roof of the cottage was a patchwork of thick wooden trellis holding the thatch, keeping out most of the weather but not the sparrows who loved to nest in it. The product of their nesting often spotted the earthen floor unless John could get up there and ring the necks of the chicks in spring. They did make a tasty addition to the pottage once undressed and gutted.

'Mrs Hargreaves let me introduce my cousin Mary and my youngest son William, and, of course, my eldest Thomas.'

Agnes came forward out of the shadow at the back of the barn. 'And this is my Agnes.' Agnes looked up and smiled, feeling awkward with everybody looking at her.

'Please have a seat at the table near the fire. Agnes, pour ale for everybody,' demanded John, sitting down at the head of the table.

Agnes, keen to be kept busy started placing the leather jacks in front of the guests, then started pouring.

When she got to Thomas, he looked up at her and she didn't know where to look. She blushed, nervously spilling some of the ale on the table.

'Don't waste it, Agnes, it's one of your mother's best batches,' John exclaimed while laughing loudly to try to ease the tension.

'Try it Thomas, tis good ale,' he said while slapping him on the back.

Thomas and William lifted the jack and took a swig. John's was almost gone by that time and gestured to Agnes for a refill. Agnes walked over and topped up the jack, then went around the other end of the table to top up the boys.

Thomas, once again looking up at her. 'Ta,' he whispered, realising that it wasn't loud enough for her to hear, coughed and thanked her again. She turned and walked over to her mother, holding the bowls for her to spoon the pottage.

'Mother, make sure Thomas gets some of that meat,' said John, demonstrating his seniority over the women in his life.

Agnes looked at her mother's facial expression as she rolled her eyes. *Is this what I am supposed to endure, erggh!* she asked herself. Agnes looked at her mother sympathetically, wondering why her father had to treat her like that when others were about.

Margaret was used to it in the company of others and didn't pay it another thought, quietly ensuring that everybody received a piece of meat in their bowl.

They all sat, Agnes opposite to Thomas and William, Margery opposite Mrs Hargreaves, John and Cousin Mary at the opposite ends of the table.

'We should say grace,' claimed John. 'Thomas, would you?' John saw it as an opportunity to pass some seniority over to Thomas. He also didn't know prayers of the Church of England.

Mrs Hargreaves and Agnes were curious because they knew he always said grace at the dinner table.

They all bowed their heads and closed their eyes except for Thomas. He kept his eyes half shut and slyly looked at Agnes. She could feel his eyes on her.

William's eyes were also half-closed, wanting to have a good look at Agnes to identify any imperfections, but there were none besides small breasts, well, smaller than the lady of disrepute up at the Kings Arms.

She had a sweet face though he thought.

Thomas began,

'Give us grateful hearts, our Father, for all thy mercies, and make us mindful of the needs of others, through Jesus Christ our Lord. Amen.'

They all repeated, 'Amen,' John making an extra effort so as not to offend and to keep his pledge made earlier that day. He was glad to have Thomas say grace, saving any embarrassment from the version that he usually used.

After they had finished the meal, Margery looked at Thomas, frowned and directed her eyes in Agnes' direction. Thomas rolled his eyes and then stood up, took a step towards Agnes who was pouring more ale. He said her name, but it didn't come out right, so he coughed and repeated it, but a bit louder than was required, 'Agnes, this is for you.' He took a step forward awkwardly, taking the posy of flowers that had wilted somewhat from behind his back and held them up to her.'

Agnes had a startled blush, not used to hearing her name coming from him. She slowly placed the tankard on the table and reached out to take the flowers, which bent over her wrist. Embarrassed by the gesture, she looked around at a room fool of silent spectators watching to see her reaction. She couldn't find the words to express herself and before she could, her mother interjected.

'How lovely, Thomas. Let's put them into some water straight away and we will dry them tomorrow as a keepsake,' said Mrs Hargreaves.

'Oh, that reminds me, I have this for you,' said Margery while placing the sweet bread she had baked especially on the table.

'Oh, that's grand,' said Mrs Hargreaves as she cut pieces and placed them in the bowls, which had been licked clean.

Agnes took polite bites of pottage, trying not to make eyes with Thomas. Thomas ate slowly, playing with his pie even though he was hungry. He felt uncomfortable in John's cottage and tried to mask his nervousness with interest and questions about the chimney. After they had finished the pie, there was an uneasy silence, none of them knowing how to commence with the business at hand.

'Agnes, take Thomas out and show him the vegetable patch, take one of those oil lamps with you,' ordered John.

Cousin Mary followed the two out the door to leave Margery and the Hargreaves to their discussion. William had another piece of sweet bread and listened with intent.

❧

Agnes walked ahead around the corner of the cottage past the animal enclosure, Thomas followed, and Mary kept about ten paces behind them. 'It's a grand night the stars are bright,' said Thomas as he looked up clumsily, trying to break the silence.

'Aye, a grand night indeed and here's the vegetable patch, carrots and the beans,' she paused, lifted the oil lantern and looked at Thomas, who smiled at the absurdity and they both laughed.

She felt more comfortable and more in control away from her father and the others, and it pleased her. It was the first time she had seen Thomas laugh and she liked it. She thought maybe this wouldn't be so bad after all.

'What do ya' think they are talking about in there?' Agnes gazed at Thomas, becoming impatient.

'There's still the dowry and the lord's coin to be arranged,' he said, sharing what he'd learnt after quizzing his mother on the way over.

'And you, is there not a young lass in the village that you're sweet on?' asked Agnes inquisitively.

He noticed how confident Agnes had become away from her father. Her green eyes sparkled in the light of the oil lamp. He observed her high cheekbones that had a bit of colour from the chilly night breeze and long eyelashes. Her skin was smooth, and her face framed by wisps of dark hair that escaped from her linen caul.

'Nooo,' he smiled, 'Not at all, too busy working in the lord's fields for such things. I saw you in the church this morning. It were brave standing up in front of the whole village,' uttered Thomas, feeling more at ease now that Agnes had spoken.

'Times are changing 'n we must all change with them,' she said wisely.

'Will you remain a Recusant Catholic and say yer payers in secret if we are to be married?'

'Nooo, I will pray to the God my husband prays to. If the lord were to find out I would lose my position at the manor or worse.'

'Anyway, enough about that. And you, is there not a fine handsome prince that comes visiting the manor that might take your fancy?'

Agnes turned away. 'Well, maybe there is and I'm just keeping my options open,' she said coyly.

'Well, Ms Hargreaves,' Thomas smiled and bowed, 'please forgive me and please don't let me stand in the way of you and your prince.'

⚘

Back in the cottage, all manner of discussions and debates were occurring between Margery and John, Mrs Hargreaves preferring to stay out of it.

'So, the way I see it, there are three or four things that we need ta discuss before a union: impediments, integrity, dowry 'n payment to the lord for marriage,' stated John in a very businesslike manner.

Margery respectfully agreed. 'Now that nasty issue with the church is out the way, is there any other reason why our Thomas shouldn't marry Agnes? Prior young ones, former betrothal, sickness of the mind?'

'No, she is as fit as a fiddle and should produce many young 'uns,' said John confidently. 'I will provide two sheep, twenty shillings, glory box and the ox for the dowry. Thomas, to make payment to the lord with the shillings, agreed?'

'Agreed,' replied Margery.

'Also, she earns 7 pennies a day at the manor, don't forget. Out of my purse into yours,' assured John. 'Oh, then there's the land, it's not much, only two acres. Having no sons, this will pass to Agnes and then to Thomas by betrothal.'

Margery smiled. 'Then it is agreed.'

⁂

Cousin Mary noticed John standing in the lit doorway of the cottage and interrupted their banter; she whispered, 'Come we must go back.' She started walking toward the door, looking back to ensure they were on their way.

Thomas followed whispering and quickly declared, 'If this does happen, just know we can start as friends, you, me and your Prince, 'n if anything else transpires, then so be it.'

Agnes turned toward the door, leaving Thomas to walk behind her. She smiled at his comment, saying nothing but knowing inside that she felt more at ease.

When the three of them walked in Cousin Mary took her seat, Thomas and Agnes remained standing, both blushing and both feeling uncomfortable, a similar feeling that they remembered from childhood when their parents found them doing wrong.

John, and in the absence of Thomas' father, Margery, stood up and approached. John Hargreaves commenced, 'Thomas Rushworth does thee agree ta have the banns read, to court Agnes for a period of one month, announce thy names and intent ta wed — on three successive Sundays at church and undergo handfasting one month from now?'

Thomas looked at Agnes who looked away, wondering what he would say.

Stuttering, 'Aye, aye, I agree,' he said.

Looking up, she turned to look at him but said nothing. His face was chiseled and weathered, his boyish good looks hardened, but still invigored and alert. Thick dark brown eyebrows crowned dark, honest, deep-set eyes. She thought he was quite handsome in a rugged sort of way.

'Hope your prince won't mind,' he whispered under his breath so that only Agnes could hear.

She turned, blushing at his remark and feeling slightly embarrassed about what she had said earlier. She gazed at her father.

'Right then, you can court my daughter,' stated John proudly.

They all clapped and cheered, John walked toward Thomas, shaking his hand and slapping him on his back.

Margery then put her hands on Agnes' upper arms and whispered into her ear, 'He's a grand bloke 'n will make a fine husband.' Margery took a step toward Thomas, grabbed him about the sides of the face, pulling his head down toward her and standing up on the tips of her toes, kissed Thomas on the forehead. She felt a sudden sadness that her dear husband wasn't there to take part, but then thought, knew, that he was probably watching from a better place. *He would have been so proud*, she thought.

William, never backward in coming forward, stood from the table, walked up to Agnes and gave her a peck on the back of the hand. 'Welcome to the family and if you ever get sick of him, take me, the better of the brothers,' he said, smirking and waiting for Thomas' reaction.

Thomas glared at William, grinned and whispered under his breath to Agnes, 'Well he better stand in line then.'

Agnes, now even more embarrassed, smiled falsely, looked to see if anybody was watching, lifted her elbow to nudge Thomas for his remark. Thomas smiled and looked ahead, giving nothing away.

The atmosphere immediately turned to one of celebration. 'Wife, Agnes, pour ale 'n cut that pie, we've somethin' ta celebrate,' said John, smiling and somewhat relieved that the serious part of the evening was over.

John took out his pipe and walked to the hearth of the fire, beckoning for Thomas to join him. He stuffed his pipe and lit a piece of straw in the fire, lifting it and shielding the flame with the palm of his hand.

He placed the flame delicately at the top of the bowl of his pipe and puffed, paused to look at the ember and puffed again, knowing the ember was a worthy one.

Thomas stood by the fire, warming himself but feeling a cold discomfort from the situation. He watched Mr Hargreaves light his pipe and was impressed by his dignity, trying to forget his indignity weeks past when they had found him. Thomas thought to himself, *who would have thought that one day we would be carrying a drunkard home and the next saying the banns for his daughter?*

'It is a funny world we live in,' Thomas whispered to himself.

'Aye it is,' said John, looking down, appreciating the fire and relishing a quiet moment.

Thomas looked into the flames then back at the ladies who were keeping themselves busy with their whispers, giggles and pretense at cleaning the mess.

Meanwhile, William was finishing the last of his pie; looking up at his big brother and Mr Hargreaves he felt out of place and awkward being the youngest. *I wonder how this will change things at home. They can't move here, two acres isn't going to support the family.*

'William is your tummy full?' asked John slightly louder than was necessary but reaffirming his right as master of the house.

'It's never full John, he could eat the horse from under his lordship's saddle,' Thomas quipped.

John laughed.

William heard the conversation and joined in the laughter. He left his empty bowl, stood and reached out to the fire to warm his hands.

CHAPTER 11

WHISPERING SWORD

It wasn't until very late they said their goodbyes and started on their way home, lighting the way with an oil lit rag wrapped around a branch. Thomas was happy with how things had gone, but he wondered if he would always feel like this. Things in his life always seem to have a way of becoming… complicated.

On their way, Thomas thought back to the discussion he had earlier with John about his layered stone and mud house with the chimney. John had told him about how there was a labour shortage because of the number of deaths from the sickness in York and that now was the perfect time to talk to the steward about building a new cottage for his mother and Agnes.

His mother wasn't getting any younger and a warmer house that kept the drafts away would better her journey into older age. It wasn't often that a parent was alive to see the marriage of their son, but he hoped it might be different this time.

William walked along, talking loudly and a bit merry from the strong ale, 'So brother have you thought about yer weddin' night yet?'

Thomas remembered what William had said to Agnes and went to grab him, but William was too fast and stepped just out of his reach. Thomas left somewhat off balance regained his footing.

'William, I am going to thump you 'till you're black and blue!' he yelled while trying to intercept his brother's run.

'You've got ta catch me first, Tommy boy.' William smiled and stayed just out of arm's reach.

Thomas was angered and put on a burst of speed that William wasn't expecting, caught him and had him in a headlock, knocking him on the top of the head with his knuckles.

'That's enough you two,' said Margery, laughing at their antics but getting weary from the walk home and the lateness of the hour.

Thomas let him go, satisfied with the punishment. 'That'll teach yer Willy boy. I can still catch ya' and give you a hidin'.'

As they walked along Moorehouse Lane, the quiet was disturbed by rustling in the bushes and Thomas stopped, holding the torch high to investigate.

Two men jumped out into the middle of the lane, their faces hidden by cloth masks and shielded by the darkness. Cousin Mary shrieked, raised her hands to her face in fright and took a step backwards. Thomas and William stepped in front of their mother protectively.

'Who do we have here then? Seems you've been celebratin',' said one of the men, his voice muffled by the mask he wore on his face. He was brandishing a sword.

'STAND AND DELIVER AND NOBODY WILL BE HURT,' yelled the other masked man, holding a knife and a truncheon, nervously moving the blade back and forth intimidatingly.

'We have no coin,' Margery said, raising her voice in the hope somebody else might hear the commotion. At that point, William ran at the masked footpad, trying to tackle him to the ground.

'NO WILLIAM!' screamed Margery as he lunged forward.

The footpad stepped, lifted his arm and brought his truncheon down on the back of William's neck. William thudded to the ground, groaning. Cousin Mary started to sob. The robber then grabbed William by the scruff of the neck, lifted him and pushed him roughly back towards the others.

'Now then, there were no need for that. If you give us your coin, you can be on your way. If not, there could be blood tonight.'

Margery stepped from behind Thomas. 'Why don't theur leave poor folk alone,' she demanded.

The footpad moved the sword from Thomas to Margery's direction. 'Well then, if you have no thought for yourself, you might have for the old wench.'

'Alright, alright leave her be,' Thomas reached into his codpiece and brought out the three shillings John had given to him to ask for the lord's blessing.

The second footpad took the coins. 'There, there, that wasn't so hard now was it? Not as poor as the old wench makes out. Right you are, all of you turn around 'n say the Lord's prayer if you turn back around before then there could be bloodshed this night!'

By the time they turned around, the footpads were long gone into the darkness across the moors. Thomas turned quickly and ran toward the edge of the trees to see if he could see them, but it was too dark, and the torch could shed light only so far.

William sat by the side of the road groaning and trying to ease the pain with his hand, rubbing the tender spot tentatively.

'Are you okay brother?'

'Let's get him home. Come on Cousin Mary, the night is a devilish one with evil creatures lurking, let's get home quickly,' said Margery worriedly.

They continued to walk home mostly in silence, except for poor William who continued to hold on to the back of his neck.

Thomas thought about the bandit. His voice sounded, well, familiar, he thought to himself, *Who were they masked men? Locals? No, couldn't be?*

When they got home, Thomas helped William to a stool, sitting him down so that Margery could have a look. She helped him take his shirt off and dabbed the red and blue that was starting to appear on his back with a wet cloth.

'Where did you get the shillings Thomas?' asked Margery inquisitively.

'John gave it to me earlier ta pay for the lord's permission for the banns.'

'Why did you fetch it with thee tonight? You know there's been footpads working here abouts,' claimed Margery angrily.

'Well, I thought ta get the lord's permission this week before next Sunday or else cop the fine for him not knowin,' pleaded Thomas.

'God help us. Where are we going ta get twenty shillings to make up the lost dowry?'

Thomas looked down, almost ready to kick himself then he looked up. 'Did you say twenty shillings? He only gave us three shillings.' They both looked at each other with relief.

'I will visit John tomorra night,' said Thomas. 'He should be told what happened.'

'Aye and you can pay a visit ta thy new young lass,' Margery went to the chest and pulled out a linen sewn handkerchief she had made. 'Give this as a gift.'

⁂

After sewing the seed all day, Margery and William, still aching from the previous night, were tired from weeding and scaring the birds so they went back to the cottage.

Thomas continued to Sun Street past the broken drywall, cottages on the left, rising hills dotted with sheep on the right. Up the hill he went where it turned into Marsh Lane. The setting sun over his left shoulder, lighting the way. Thomas finally reached the top of the hill and let his legs carry him down the other side. Down he went, past more cottages, Moorhouse Lane, across the field and there it was. The Hargreaves stone cottage, cattle door open; the light of the fire escaping through the shutter.

The dogs barked. 'John are you there? It is I, Thomas,' he called out. Agnes appeared in the light of the door.

'Father is away, but mother is here. It is grand ta see thee,' said Agnes, pleased with his visit.

Thomas had noticed she had taken off her Sunday best, but she still looked pretty in the working clothes she wore. He could see the gravy stain on her apron where she had been mixing and the flour still in her hair from the manor kitchen. He had never seen her with her hair out and he was impressed, long and dark with a slight wave which added to the shine.

'I must speak to your father; we were robbed last night on the way home. William was hurt, two footpads brandishing swords and bludgeons. They threatened mother and stole shillings your father gave me.'

Mrs Hargreaves looked over. 'Is William alright? John is out tending to the crop but you're welcome to stay and wait for him, sit by the fire. Agnes, pour Thomas an ale.'

Thomas sat at the form near the fire as Mrs Hargreaves had instructed. Agnes poured ale and walked over, handing it to Thomas who looked up at her.

Agnes blushed. 'Would you like something to eat? We have the pottage from last night and some good dark bread I made this morning, I brought it back from the manor.'

'Will you sit with me for a while?' asked Thomas, shuffling over to make room for her.

Agnes looked over at her mother for approval, who looked away, letting Agnes make her own decision.

She sat, feeling far more comfortable than last night. They didn't say a thing, just enjoyed each other's company. Staring into the fire, they both seemed mesmerised by the dancing flames. That was until the dogs started barking and Agnes could hear her father approaching. She immediately stood up, feeling self-conscious and trying to overcompensate by walking toward the door. 'Father, Thomas is here, he has bad news.'

'So I can see,' said John, not used to having other men in his house when he arrived home.

He took off his hat and hung it on the nail. 'So what is this bad news Thomas?' he enquired.

'We were robbed by two footpads on the way home last night. They belted William and made off with the three shillings that you gave me.'

'Sard,' exclaimed John with an angry contempt, not for Thomas, but for the brutes who got away with the three shillings. 'That's the second time!'

Both Mrs Hargreaves and Agnes were taken aback by this because they rarely heard their father swear. 'Please husband sit and have your tea, what is done is done,' pleaded his wife sympathetically.

'Tomorrow we will both go to the manor to ask for an audience with the steward and report these brutes!' exclaimed John.

'Tonight, you can stay here; we will go first thing in the mornin'.' Agnes brought over a bowl of pottage and tankard of ale for her father at the table and a tankard of ale for Thomas.

Agnes sat down beside him. 'Are you okay Thomas?' she enquired.

'Times are hard enough without all this,' Thomas said sadly.

'No use in crying over spilt milk, at least William is okay,' she whispered wisely. 'Are you still in the frame of mind that you were last night? Any doubts?' She looked at him inquisitively.

'No doubts at all,' said Thomas confidently. 'And you and your prince?'

She smiled and lightly elbowed him.

Then he remembered, 'Oh, I have something for you.' Standing, he reached into his tunic and handed Agnes the linen handkerchief. 'I hope you like it.'

'Oh, nobody has ever given me anything so beautiful before,' said Agnes, blushing.

'The pattern is fine, such intricate work and the colour of that rose, so beautiful,' she held it up to the fire to inspect the stitching.

'Are you nervous about saying the banns on Sunday?' she asked worriedly.

'It's my duty,' said Thomas. 'I will build us a house made of mud and layered stone, with a chimney and a thatch roof. When you are ready, we will have children, many children,' stated Thomas in a mature, demanding tone.

Agnes looked at him, raising her eyebrows, 'Will we now? Do I not get a say in these plans of yours?' she asked cheekily.

Embarrassed, Thomas realised he had overstepped the mark. 'Please forgive me, I have insulted you,' he looked down and shuffled his feet.

'Not at all,' claimed Agnes. 'I was just wondering whether you wanted my help or if I was to just lie there in the mud and layered stone house,' she grinned, enjoying toying with him.

Feeling guilty and looking defensive, Thomas started to try to explain himself, 'Agnes, I only meant…'

Agnes liked his naivety, she smiled, then he realised she was goading him. He shook his head. 'That was mean.'

'Why was it mean?' she asked, still smiling.

'Because I thought I'd insulted you,' he claimed, looking down at the gravel floor, shuffling his feet. He felt inexperienced in the ways of women.

John and his wife were sitting at the table facing away from them, John looked back to see Agnes smiling and Thomas saddened for some reason. 'What is going on?'

'Well, Agnes is smiling, so I wouldn't worry,' grumbled Mrs Hargreaves.

'Ayup, how do ya' know she's smiling wife? You haven't turned around to look since the last bells.'

'I don't need ta turn around husband, I see things perfectly well.'

'Wife don't say things like that or else thee will be labelled a witch,' John whispered.

Mrs Hargreaves looked down at the table and tapped the knife that she used to gut fish and smiled. Holding it up at an angle with the blade's edge resting on the table, she could see the reflection of Agnes and Thomas by the fire.

'Wife, sometimes you are too cunning for thy own good,' John laughed that laugh when he was really amused. The laugh where his head rolled back and his stomach pumped in and out, and the holes of his missing teeth were visible for all to see.

Agnes noticed his peculiar jocularity. 'Father, what is it?' It was rare that she saw him in such good spirits, especially after a full day in the fields. It pleased her.

'Agnes, I just remarked to your mother how good she is with the blade, you know, gutting fish and all that.'

Mrs Hargreaves stood up from the table. 'Right you two it's time for bed; Agnes get out the mattress.'

Thomas stood up from the bench and started to walk toward the animal fixture at the back of the cottage.

'And where do you think you're going Master Thomas?' Mrs Hargreaves called out stubbornly. 'You get right back here, you will not be sleeping with the animals tonight,' she said confidently as she reached for her sewing kit.

Agnes threw down the straw-filled mattress and disappeared into the corner of the cottage to disrobe and brush the flour from her hair, a nightly ritual.

Mrs Hargreaves threw a linen blanket on the bed. 'Lie down here Thomas,' she instructed.

Thomas felt awkward. 'Mrs Hargreaves,' he muddled his words, 'I don't think this is, well, right and proper.'

Embarrassed, he looked over at Mr Hargreaves who had poured himself another ale and sat there smiling his gummy grin.

'Now, doff thy hose and tunic,' she demanded, helping him untie. Thomas looked around for Agnes; she was absent. *Thank goodness,* he thought.

Mr Hargreaves continued to drink his ale in front of the fire and watched the commotion. He tried not to laugh.

'Mrs Hargreaves, this is right peculiar,' said Thomas as she helped him undress, pulling his hose by the bottom, lifting his buttocks right off the mattress.

Thomas grabbed for his undershirt, ensuring it covered his nether regions.

'Don't you be too concerned about that Thomas Rushworth, seen it all, nothing you got that me two sons didn't have.'

Mrs Hargreaves was saddened by the thought, but relished the idea of having another young male in the house. It brought back golden memories and disturbing ones that she pushed from her mind.

When Agnes returned, she looked like an angel. She had a pure white linen undershirt on that hung to her knees. Her long hair had been brushed, the flour was gone, and it shone like silk. She had washed her face with cold water that had brought a rosy colour back to her cheeks. Her nipples were erect from the draught, slightly visible through the linen because of the light of the fire.

She laid down beside Thomas, not saying a thing but smirking seeing him there in the light of the fire, bundled up in a linen sheet. Mrs Hargreaves had sewn the outer two edges together with thick string at the front and folded up the bottom and sewn it shut. The front had been neatly sewn to the edge of material at the back over his shoulders. The only thing visible was Thomas' head sticking out of the cocoon-like garment.

He could barely move and had a look of resentment on his face. He dared not say anything, but he could feel the tiny creatures starting to move about his crotch. He tried to scratch, but didn't want to arouse any suspicion about what he was doing under the cover.

A minute later, Agnes lying beside him eyes open, stared up into the darkness and moved her hand closer to feel Thomas' hand through the linen. Thomas opened his eyes, staring up into the darkness too reciprocated. They both laid there in silence for a while until Mr Hargreaves belched, passed wind and then started snoring.

Agnes giggled and whispered, 'Welcome to the family.' She rolled over and tried to go to sleep.

Thomas, feeling the bedbugs running over his chest and the fleas itching his crotch, smiled in contentment, closed his eyes and laid there all night not sleeping a wink. Agnes didn't move at all for some time, and he could hear her slow, relaxed breaths. When she did turn over, he could only see the outline of her face in the darkness, wisps of breath touched the side of his face and he wished it was lighter so he could see her rosy complexion up close.

The next morning, Agnes got up, went to the back of the cottage, dressed and went outside while Thomas was released from his bundling by John using his wife's gutting knife. Mr Hargreaves approaching with a knife was not a pleasant experience, especially after spending the night lying beside his only daughter.

Mrs Hargreaves was already up and completing the morning chores. The sun was not up yet, but the household was in full swing. Mr Hargreaves led the cow and ox out to the common green. Mrs Hargreaves ushered the four sheep out of their keep attached to the back of the cottage. Thomas donned his hose, tunic and jerkin and adjusted his codpiece quickly before they came back inside.

A few minutes later, Mr Hargreaves returned and walked through the door, wet from the Yorkshire drizzle that had just started. 'Did theur sleep well Thomas?'

'Aye John, warm as a bug in the rug,' he said, thinking about the bed bug bite marks on his chest and the itch from the fleas that were imprisoned with him for the night. He scratched.

Mrs Hargreaves smiled at the pun, knowing that he was referring to the sleeping attire that she had provided.

Mr Hargreaves looked at Thomas with a serious look on his face, 'I'm going to do some weeding 'till the sun is fully risen, then I'll meet you at your cottage; we can go to the manor together.'

'Ahl be off then, sithee later. Where is Agnes?' enquired Thomas.

'Oh, she's long gone to the manor lest she be fined or whipped for being late,' answered Mrs Hargreaves.

'You can come back around t'night if theur like. We can make you as warm as a bug in a rug again.'

Thomas grinned, realising she had picked up on his attempt at humour. 'Right, tarreur then,' said Thomas as he opened the cattle door and walked through.

On his way home, he thought about last night and he felt warm and content, as if a large weight had been removed from his shoulders. He remembered how Agnes had touched his hand affectionately through the linen bundling and smiled; then he frowned, thinking about the new responsibility that he had to care and support her. His mind started to get all jumbled up with worries. *What if she wasn't a good wife? What if they couldn't have children? What if there was a drought and he couldn't provide for her and the young ones?* He tried hard to dismiss the thoughts and concentrate on the job at hand, weeding the field and going to the manor.

When he arrived home, Margery and William were already out in the fields. They were both wet and miserable from the continued drizzle but were happy to see Thomas lend a hand. Weeding and looking for pests on ten acres was a challenge.

'And where have you been young Thomas?' asked Margery. 'Is your own family not good enough for you anymore that you must stay out to all hours?'

William, less sore from his argument with the truncheon added, 'He's been kanoodling with Agnes, mother, I wouldn't expect much effort from him thereabouts.'

'Shut up William!' shouted Thomas as the drizzle started to turn into larger droplets and run down his face.

Thomas picked up a hessian bag laying on the ground, walked along the valley beside the seedlings, pulling the chickweed and charlock from the ground.

'William, you must accompany Mr Hargreaves and I to the manor later, we are going to report last night's happenings to the steward.'

'And a lot it will do too,' grumbled William. 'They are long gone by now!'

'I'm not so sure about that.'

'It doesn't matter William, still has to be reported for the good of the village,' said Margery, getting a cold shiver down her back from the coldness of her soaked kirtle.

The three of them remained silent as they trudged along in the relentless rain, occasionally stopping, standing upright to ease the stiffness in their back.

A ribbon of bright orange was the only indication of the start of sunrise. It burst through the dense cloud, trying hard not to be swallowed up by the sky. The birds started to make their morning song, silhouettes against the grey curtain of cloud. Some of them flew down to the field to get an early morning feed of worms that had ventured out of the damp ground. The Pennine moors shone under the enlarging orange beam of light that started to creep up the sky.

Margery, Thomas and William made their way back up the hill, hessian bags full and thrown over their shoulder, their woolen clothes soaked through as they shivered. Their woolen and hide foot coverings were caked with mud and slippery underfoot, forcing Thomas to lend a hand to his mother.

They opened the door and walked in, William shivered and sneezed. Thomas walked straight to the hearth and put another log on the fire, then stood there holding his hands out to the radiant heat. They all undressed, taking everything off except their undershirts. Margery hung their clothes over a piece of string that had been nailed from one side of the room to the other for just that purpose. They sat down on stools around the hearth, trying to warm themselves. Neither said a word just pleased to be out of it. They only had two sets of clothing, so they dried themselves and waited for their clothes to dry.

Thomas looked out the shutter. The drizzle had started to subside, and the sun painted a rainbow over the red, green and brown of the moors. The cloud broke, and the sun shone on the lustrous green of the long strip of farrow fields. The rest, a hundred dark squares on a chessboard waiting for the seed to germinate and turn them green. William was the first to notice Mr Hargreaves walking toward the house. He was muddy and wet, and by the looks of it in no mood for trivialities.

'Ayup there anybody at home?' he cried out so as not to startle the family.

'Come in John, dry yourself by the fire. Wicked morning, but it's grand for the seedlings. God willing, we will have a good harvest this summer,' said Margery. 'Thomas and William come, sit by the fire, let's plan the strategy for battle.'

'Battle? Are we to take weapons John?' enquired William sarcastically.

'No, not weapons William, just words,' replied Thomas wisely.

John smiled at Thomas, impressed with his foresight and wisdom. John went on to explain that there were three reasons for the audience with the steward, the first was to ask for permission for Thomas' union to Agnes, the second was to ask for permission to build a new cottage on the hide and the third was to report the abuse of the village residents and misuse of the king's highways by marauders and footpads.

He wasn't to know at the time, but these three simple requests were going to be a lot more difficult than he thought.

'I'll do the talking and offer the shillings for the banns for you and Agnes,' John looked at Thomas.

'Young William, just stay quiet and offer a look at the bruise on thy back if I command you ta do so, understand?' He looked at William.

All three walked out through the cattle door. Margery watched them walk out then put her head down and continued making the dough for bread. She realised that there were circumstances best left to menfolk, and she trusted Mr Hargreaves.

CHAPTER 12

TIME OF SERVANTS

They walked around the back of the manor; the reeve was there receiving vegetables from one of the village folk.

'Ayeup John, Thomas, young William, what brings theur to the manor?'

'There's been trouble, and we wish ta speak to the steward,' said John.

'Emmm,' the reeve paused. 'Theur can't cum knocking on the lord's door every time there's a bit of trouble in the village.'

John tried to convince the reeve. 'It's not just trouble, both myself 'n William have been assaulted. Lord's shillings were robbed. They were to be paid to the lord for father's funeral,' Thomas explained, making it sound as if it were the lord's money that had been robbed and it was he that was out of pocket.

'Alright then. Well, you better hold on here,' said the reeve as he turned and disappeared through the back door. He appeared a few moments later. 'You better come with me.'

They all took off their hats and walked through the large oak door into the kitchen; it was hustle and bustle of activity with three servant girls and a cook busily preparing the lord's lunch and dinner. Large bubbling pots hung underneath a vast stone chimney that stretched almost the entire width of the room. Steam and smoke from the fire ascended and then disappeared up the chimney.

Thomas and William were in awe of the size of the room, both looking up and turning their heads to take in the magnificence of the structure. When they both looked forward, they noticed Agnes standing at a large table, plucking brightly coloured feathers from a pheasant. She was surprised to see them. She smiled but didn't stop what she was doing for fear of being scolded by the cook. Thomas noticed the assortment of breads and bowls on the table, but he was most astonished by the amount of meat drying on racks over the fire. William also noticed the beef, chicken, lamb and pork and he started to salivate from the aroma. At the other end of the room was a large pantry filled with all manner of vegetables, fruit, eggs and hanging birds. Another small room to the side contained another fire and table, covered with flour for making the dough and cooking bread. There was a large serving opening through which the dishes were passed to be served to the lord in another room. Beside this was another opening through which the reeve walked, and the visitors followed. Thomas took one more look back to see Agnes looking at him. He turned to the front as the reeve opened the large oak door to the great hall.

John, William, then Thomas followed the reeve into the great hall; John walked forward, but William and Thomas stopped and looked up into the roof trusses twenty odd feet above their heads. The room must have been thirty-five feet in length and over half that in breadth. At the end of the hall was a tall, narrow window capped by a sharply pointed arch and another clerestory window at the side; the sun was streaming in to light the room. There was wood paneling on the far wall and an entrance to a small chapel with a table and a cross. Opposite the clerestory window there was a fireplace and a high chimney. In the middle of the room, opposite the fire, was a large table where the lord sat. The steward was whispering to the lord as John approached, then stood upright and stepped back.

John strolled up to the table and dipped his head. 'My Lord.'

Thomas caught up and stood beside him, William a step back. 'Lord Birkhead.' Thomas dipped his head, as did William.

'Thomas Rushworth, I knew of your dear old father, he was a good man. I'm sorry to hear of his sickness and passing,' said the lord in the King's English. 'John Hargreaves, one's steward, tells me that there has been skulduggery about. What have you to report?'

'Aye, my Lord, two footpads robbed Thomas and assaulted his brother William on the road ta Haworth on Moorehouse Lane. His mother were threatened with a sword and thy coin for the Rushworth funeral were robbed,' reported John.

The steward, trying to convince the lord of foul play, leant forward and whispered in his ear, 'My Lord, they are giving excuses for failure to pay.'

'John Hargreaves, when the coin was supposedly stolen it was not in my possession, so Thomas Rushworth is still indebted. Furthermore, how is one to know that this isn't all a concocted story to delay payment?'

'Maybe time in the pillory will ensure more prompt payment, my Lord,' added the steward looking at Thomas.

'My Lord, there is no need. We came here ta inform theur of the shenanigans hereabouts. I were assaulted 'n left for dead not two weeks ago in the same area by two men I befriended at the Kings Arms.'

Still trying to convince his lordship, John turned to William. 'Then there's this. William, come forward, lift thy shirt.'

William took a step forward, turned and lifted his shirt, showing a large purple and red bruise on his upper back. He pulled his shirt down and returned to his place. The lord beckoned the steward closer. 'Did you know of this steward?'

The steward leant to whisper, trying to discredit the men that stood before them, remembering the night of the manor court, 'No my Lord, but I have seen these peasants drunk and disorderly thereabouts.'

'Emm, the two footpads that robbed you, were they locals? What did they look like?' enquired the lord. 'Had you seen them before?'

Thomas stepped in. 'Begging thy pardon my Lord, it was dark 'n their faces were covered.'

Lord Birkhead raised his voice, 'Do you know about this steward? Goodness me, I pay you to tend to business in the village.'

'Yes, my Lord, I know about it.'

John placed coin on the table. 'My Lord, I have three shillings for thy permission for my daughter Agnes ta wed young Thomas Rushworth and another for the funeral for Thomas Rushworth, may he rest in peace.'

'No John, that is my debt,' whispered Thomas.

John whispered under his breath, 'Don't worry lad, all will be well.'

John had forfeited his land at the previous parish, due to his recusancy, but still had a comfortable sum left over after the purchase of the three acres at Oxenhope. This they had been living off, but it would not last forever.

'Steward have the clerk take notice of the payment of John Hargreaves and Thomas Rushworth and inform the night watchman and the deputies of the robbery and assault, Heavens above!'

The steward picked up the coin, turned, dipped his head at the lord and walked across the hall and through the door. His steps echoing as he walked.

'There is one other matter my Lord. Thomas would like ta build a mud and layered stone cottage with a chimney ta keep his family warm through the winter.'

The lord, knowing of the labour shortage because of the Black Death, granted permission for the cottage and bid them farewell.

They dipped their heads, turned, and walked across the hall and back out the door into the kitchen. Thomas was keen to set eyes on Agnes, but she was nowhere to be seen. They walked through the kitchen, taking one more look at the food being prepared. Thomas turned to John while they were walking, 'I don't know how ta thank you John.'

'No thanks necessary. It is I that should thank you for sparing me on that fateful night. Only God knows what would have happened if you and thy mother hadn't come along.

'Seems that the alehouse is the root of all the trouble,' stated John, deep in thought about his night of condemnation. 'Two footpads robbed you and two men that assaulted me the night you found me; could they be one and the same?'

The steward walked into the Kings Arms alarmed at the sharpness of the smell of urine and stale ale; he put his hand up to his mouth and coughed. Two men sat on three-legged stools using a cut barrel as a gaming table. Their swords wrapped with a large black belt leant against the wall behind them. The steward walked up to them and sat down, and they dealt him into the game. The steward picked up the cards, but there was more than the game on his mind.

'Two men from the village have met with the lord and told him of a robbery on Moorhouse Lane the other night.'

His companions looked at each other then back at the steward. The steward placed two shillings on the table, his acquaintances picked them up and placed them in their coin purse. 'Until things calm down, return ta Stanbury. Come back on Sunday for the rat baiting,' commanded the steward.

His two companions placed their cards on the table, stood up and walked to the door. The last one to leave took one last look back before walking out into the day.

Thomas and Agnes sat together in church for the first time. They sat in a pew with Margery on one side of them and John on the other. William, Mrs Hargreaves and Cousin Mary sat in front for moral support.

After the sermon, the vicar coughed and proceeded to read out the announcements from the lectern, 'By the power of our Lord Jesus Christ our saviour and our sovereign, King James the first of England and Scotland, I herewith announce the banns of marriage between Thomas Rushworth, son of Thomas and Margery, of Haworth and Agnes

Hargreaves, daughter of John and Margaret of Oxenhope. This is the first time of asking. If any of you know cause or just impediment why these two persons should not be joined together in Holy Matrimony, yee are to declare it.'

Thomas and Agnes touched hands and looked at each other, then forward as the congregation now had their eyes upon them.

'Now let us pray.'

'Lord, the source of all true love, we pray for this couple. Grant to them joy of heart, seriousness of mind and reverence of spirit, that as they enter into the oneness of marriage, they may be strengthened and guided by you, through Jesus Christ our Lord. Amen.'

'Amen,' the congregation repeated in unison.

'Lord of love, we pray for Thomas and Agnes, be with them in all their preparations and on their wedding day. Give them your love in their hearts throughout their married life together, through Jesus Christ our Lord. Amen.'

'Amen.'

Margery and the rest of the congregation awaited the news.

The vicar spoke, 'I have news from Windsor Castle, our sovereign King James of England and Scotland has proclaimed that England and Scotland will unite under his crown.'

'Our sovereign has forbidden any Londoners and other inhabitants of places infected with the Black Death to come to court. He has also proclaimed that gentlemen of court should depart for the country to escape the ravages of the Black Death, which has devastated so many in London and York.'

The parishioners whispered excitedly.

The vicar raised his hands. 'Finally, he has decreed the execution of former laws against Catholic Recusants, giving them a day to repair to their dwellings and not afterward to come to the court or within 10 miles of London without special license.

'There is also a reward for the arrest and capture of the traitor Thomas Percy for his thwarted attempt of the devastation of Parliament.

'God save the King.'

'God save the King,' they repeated.

The congregation filed out of the church.

John Hargreaves called out, 'Thomas 'n William! Fancy a celebratory ale at the Kings Arms while we're up here?'

Thomas was more interested in spending more time with Agnes, but he didn't want to disappoint his future father-in-law, especially after he just paid his debts. He watched on as Agnes, Mrs Hargreaves and Margery continued to walk toward Sun Street and down the hill toward home.

CHAPTER 13

THE OBSESSION WITH THE STARS

Thomas and William followed Mr Hargreaves into the alehouse. The shutters were open, and a stream of sunlight burst in. The heat from the sunlight caused a ripple of putrid steam to emanate from the ground. A chamber pot sat in the corner, still not emptied from the previous night. The room was full, handicraftsmen, workers of all sorts, labourers, cobblers, pedlars and porters. Other poor folk drank the swill from the jacks left behind and begged for coins. The maidservant dropped jacks of ale to the different tables, her bosom accentuated by the open front of her blouse.

William couldn't divert his eyes.

The maidservant noticed him staring and sauntered over to him. She leant over and whispered in his ear, 'Looking is free, but touching will cost ya'.'

Thomas was listening to John but watching William and the maidservant flirting. Her large bosom accentuated by the tight drawstring across her chest.

'It seems that any strange goings on has links with this establishment. They must frequent this tavern or at least get information about the goings on from somebody local.'

'This tavern,' Thomas agreed. 'Whoever it is they would have heard about your winnings that night and heard about mine and Agnes' commitment to the banns. They would have known about the dowry!'

John peered at Thomas, who was transfixed by what was happening behind his back; he turned to see William, his eyes fixated on the bosom of the serving wench. She was still bent over, bosom at William's eye level, giving him a good look at her pushed up cleavage. John lifted his leg and placed his foot on her behind and gave her a mighty push, which sent her reeling across the room.

'Be off with you foul mistress, play thy seduction games with another,' said John protectively. The maidservant, angrier about losing a potential customer than the physicality, gathered herself, straightened her wimple and moved on.

The door opened and the reeve from the manor walked in. 'Ayup John, Thomas, William, all the best with the banns Thomas,' he had heard them read out at the Church of Saint Michael All Angels that morning.

'What keeps you in deep discussion?' asked the reeve. 'I heard about the trouble on Moorhouse Lane. These are desperate times 'n desperate times make desperate men,' he said wisely.

'It seems that any trouble that occurs near the village has links with this alehouse,' whispered John.

'Then you best speak to the steward; he oversees the place for Lord Birkhead.'

'The steward overseas the alehouse?' asked Thomas.

'Aye, has done for years, organises the entertainment downstairs in the basement as well,' he remarked as he picked up the jack that the maidservant had dumped on the table. She gave John a look of disdain.

The reeve always made sure that he was honest and straight forth with the tenants of the lord's demesne, as it was them that voted him in at the festival of Michaelmas. When the lord and the steward was away, he had the run of the place, a position that he had held for several years.

'Can't speak ta him now though he's away in Stanbury, should be back tomorra. In his absence you could speak ta his deputies, one of them is sitting over there.' The reeve pointed to three men sitting at a table across the room.

Thomas approached the table, none of the men looked up. 'Your grace, I have urgent business ta report.'

The deputy was looking at his cards; it was apparent that he was losing as the other two gentlemen had small piles of coin in front of them, whereas his part of the table was void of any. '

'Can't you see I'm busy lad?' claimed the deputy, refusing to look up. He placed his hand down on the table and waited for his two companions to do the same. One of the others placed his cards on the table, grinned and collected the remaining coins.

'Sard, that's it, I'm out,' stated the deputy angrily.

'Right lad, what's this business you need ta report so urgently that theur interrupt the card games?'

'Would you be so kind as to join me and my companions?' Thomas held out his hand and ushered the deputy toward John and William. The reeve stood up and encouraged the deputy to be seated.

'Greetings,' said John as they all sat back down again, 'This is William Rushworth and I am John Hargreaves, you know the reeve.' The reeve dipped his head and left, not wanting to get too involved in deep discussion with the deputy.

'Aye, I know who you are. I heard about the trouble you had on Moorhouse Lane t'other night,' said the deputy.

He put on a serious face. 'Sounds ta me like footpads from out of town, maybe those coney-catchers seeking retribution.'

'And I heard theur had trouble of thy own John Hargreaves,' enquired the deputy.

The deputy looked around the tavern, 'I'll wager it is the same two rogues that caused thy misfortune. From Stanbury or Oxenhope, can't see it being one of the locals. Unfortunately, we can't do much unless we cop them in the act.'

'Seems both incidents may have something ta do with the alehouse,' stated John, as he sat forward and whispered.

'How do you figure?' asked the deputy, staring at Thomas. 'It is his grace, the steward, who oversees this place. Did theur not see the fine job he did apprehending the coney-catchers on the night of the manor court?'

'Aye, ah did,' whispered Thomas. 'But it is too much of a coincidence, John was assaulted after the rat baiting. Where would one hear of our betrothal? Everybody in here knew of it!'

'I think you are barking up the wrong tree, it were the steward who reported the trouble on behalf of the lord. If he or the householder were involved, why would he report it? I'd be careful if I were you before you all end up in the pillory for slandering,' the deputy warned.

John looked at the deputy worriedly.

'The manor court is in session next week; I will keep an eye out. In the meantime, I suggest you quieten thy wayward ideas, lest me and my partner come knocking on your door. We are under the steward's orders to catch these bastards so let us do our job.'

The deputy stood and walked to the bar to get another tankard of ale. The householder poured from the barrel and placed it in front of him.

'What were all that about?' asked the householder inquisitively. He liked to keep abreast of any news.

'Oh, just a private matter,' said the deputy, having been in the job long enough to know not to fill other's ears. He picked up his pewter tankard and walked back to the card table in the corner of the room.

A week had passed, and once again, Thomas and Agnes sat together in church. The congregation seemed to have adjusted to them sitting together, and nobody had declared illegitimacy to their union.

'By the power of the Lord Jesus Christ our saviour and our sovereign King James the first of England and Scotland, I herewith announce the banns of marriage between Thomas Rushworth, son of Thomas and Margery, of Haworth and Agnes Hargreaves, daughter of John and Margaret of Oxenhope. This is the second time of asking, if any of you know cause or just impediment why these two persons should not be joined together in Holy Matrimony, ye are to declare it.'

Margery awaited news, the vicar cleared his throat and spoke from the lectern, 'I have news from Windsor Castle, our sovereign Lord King James of England and Scotland has proclaimed the authorisation and uniformity of the book of common prayer and enjoying conformity to the form of the service of God now established.'

'God save the King.'

The churchgoers repeated in unison, 'God save the King.' Then filed out of the church and went their separate ways.

Thomas, John and William walked ahead of the womenfolk. Thomas was deep in thought about the deputy's words, and the idea of being locked in the pillory gave him cold shivers down his back.

'I go to the manor court during the week, best go and be spared the lord's fine,' Thomas claimed.

'Thomas, why don't theur come back ta ours for supper? We'll travel together to the manor court. Safer that way,' John claimed.

'Aye, but I have work to do first; animals need tending and peat needs collecting,' explained Thomas.

Margery heard and interrupted, 'Gew on son, nowt that William and I can't do. Spend time with thy Agnes. Won't be long before the harvest and then it will be all hands to the sickle.'

Agnes didn't let on, but had hoped Thomas would visit again. They had been so busy in the fields that it had seemed like weeks since they had talked. She spent most of her day at the manor and any free time with her mother and father, weeding so that the young shoots of wheatgrass had a chance to grow.

'Right, you are, then. Agnes, does thee have any objections?' asked Thomas.

Agnes caught up to him, John and William walked ahead, and

Margery and Mrs Hargreaves walked ten paces behind, slowing down so that the two could have their privacy but still be in earshot of the conversation. Both Thomas and Agnes both started to say something, and both stopped to allow the other to say what they were going to say. They both laughed.

'You go on,' said Thomas politely.

Agnes smiled. 'Can't believe it's only one more week ta go till the handfasting.'

'Still no doubts?' enquired Thomas.

'No, none,' she replied then grinned.

Thomas frowned. 'What you grinnin' about?'

'I remember when mother first mentioned it, I were dead against it. I had visions of you beating me 'n sending me to the ducking stool.'

'Them laws can go on too far. I say, would the Lord do it thusly? Fear not Agnes Hargreaves, you are safe with me,' replied Thomas.

They walked in silence for a while, just enjoying being at each other's side. Soon after, William and Margery turned toward home and the others continued to Moorhouse Lane, stopping briefly where the footpads had robbed them.

Thomas noticed something at the side of the road clinging to a piece of blackberry bramble. 'Ayup, what's this?' he asked, trying to wrestle it away from the thorns of the bush.

His hose got caught in the bramble, so he let out an almighty yelp, refusing to move until he had untangled himself.

Agnes became impatient. 'Come on Thomas, let's get home.'

'It's a piece of a sleeve from somebody's undershirt, could belong to one of the footpads that robbed us. Look John, it were about here where they jumped from their hiding place.'

John turned and walked back, taking the small piece of cloth in his hand. 'Could be, but doubt it. There are fifty that walk past this bramble every day.'

'You're probably right,' Thomas took the cloth looking disappointed and put it in his cod piece for later inspection.

Thomas and Agnes walked up to the cottage and sat on a wooden bench near the cattle door. They allowed the sun to shine on their faces. The bright green of the growing wheat sparkled on the hills, further accentuated by the beige, pinks and brown hues of the moor.

Mrs Hargreaves walked out to them and gave them both a jack of ale. 'It's a beautiful day,' she said, stopping to appreciate it then stepping back inside the cottage.

'Thy mother is a prize of a woman,' said Thomas.

'She has had a difficult life, lost two boys 'n two girls, two at birth, two within five years because of the sickness. Father were crushed,' Agnes started to tear up.

'Ah, I'm sorry Agnes,' he put his arm around her, until he heard Mrs Hargreaves cough then took it away again.

'Come Agnes.' He took her by the hand. Mrs Hargreaves coughed again, so he let go.

They walked to the wood and wattle enclosed vegetable garden. 'Right you are. You see that large branch in the fence at the bottom of the garden there? I wager I can hit it two out of three times with any stone that you pick,' joked Thomas.

'That's impossible, but if it's a wager, what are we wagering on?' asked Agnes.

'Well, if I lose, I will do thy weeding for a day. But I'm not gonna lose,' he said cheekily. 'And if I win?'

'Aye, what if you win? Though I doubt it unless a miracle happens here in Oxenhope.

Well, what do you want? I have nowt.'

'Simple, a kiss,' Thomas hesitated then grinned, waiting for the inevitable retribution.

'Thomas Rushworth, do you want ta see my mother come screaming with the broom ta see thee off and my father ta have thy guts for garters?' she said alarmingly, but then quietened as her mother appeared at the door.

'Well, you say I can't do it, so what's to worry Ms Agnes Hargreaves?'

'I think you presume too much, Thomas Rushworth,' she said while looking for a stone.

Thomas took the stone in his hand, squinted his eye and threw it, hitting the branch at its centre almost twenty paces away.

Agnes was stunned. 'You've done this before, Thomas. Is this how you get girls from the village ta kiss thee? By throwing stones at a twig?'

'Nah, William and I used ta have throwing contests ta see who had ta shovel out the animal enclosure.'

She looked around for another stone, one that would swing the wager in her favour. She found one almost half the size of a man's fist. 'There you go, try this one,' she said smartly while placing it in Thomas' hand.

'Agnes, this is unfair. This is not a stone,' he said, sizing up its weight and the distance that he had to throw it. 'Am I that foul that a kiss would be punishment for thee?'

'Lower your voice and just stick to the wager,' she said, ignoring all other suggestions and consequences.

Thomas took the stone in his right hand, squinted his eye and threw it, but it landed a foot too short.

'Seems like the wager is lost Thomas Rushworth. I'll leave the hessian bag for thee,' she said smugly while looking for another stone even more difficult to throw than the last.

'There you go,' she said boldly, trying not to demoralise her young suitor too harshly.

She found a stone, quartz, rough and peculiar looking. And started to feel sympathy for Thomas, but stayed on course as she knew this was not a test of love, but a test of wits.

She handed the stone to Thomas who looked at it and smiled. 'Agnes, you are too cunning for thy own good.' He sized up its weight and the distance that he had to throw it; he looked at her, then back at the target.

Impatiently, Agnes rolled her eyes. 'Thomas, in God's name just throw it.'

Thomas took one last look at the stone and one last look at the target, brought his hand back confidently, then walked past Agnes down the side of the vegetable garden and turned to face her.

Agnes frowned. 'Thomas, what on earth are you doing?'

Thomas raised his voice, 'If you remember Agnes, the wager were ta hit the twig twice out of three times with any stone that ya' pick. I said nowt about throwing the stone.

'Seems like the wager is lost, Ms Agnes Hargreaves.' He had his back to the twig, released the stone, hitting the twig right in the middle.

All this time, Mr and Mrs Hargreaves had been peeking through the gap between the shutter and the wall, giggling.

Thomas placed the stone in his codpiece then walked back up the garden.

Angry that she had been fooled so easily, she said, 'Seems you have me at a disadvantage, Thomas Rushworth.'

'Disadvantage, advantage, ah suppose it depends on the way you look at it.'

John heard the bell of Saint Michael of All Angels, realising the time he called out, 'Thomas, it's time to get on our way say your goodbyes.'

Agnes was stunned by the sound of her father's voice, as if it woke her from a dream.

'It seems like it is time for you to go,' Agnes said as Thomas walked up the side of the garden to say farewell.

He stood facing her. He could tell that his prank still perturbed her; he held her hands in his. Knowing that she had her back to the cottage door, he leant forward. She closed her eyes and relaxed, her lips almost in a pout for what seemed like an eternity; she opened her eyes.

Thomas released her hands. 'It has been a pleasure spending time with you this afternoon Agnes, I hope we might do it again sometime.'

Grinning, he joined John as he walked out the cottage door.

Stunned, Agnes turned angrily as Thomas walked away. 'THOMAS

RUSHWORTH, YOU ARE... ERRGH...' she growled and grunted then marched off toward the cottage.

John watched Agnes storm off in contempt. 'I see you have been getting ta know my daughter. She can have a wild spirit when she wants ta,' he said.

'Aye I've noticed,' replied Thomas.

CHAPTER 14

THE SOULS OF SILVER

John and Thomas continued walking in silence across the fields, down Moorhouse Lane onto Manor Lane to Sun Street. A beautiful evening, the knee-high wheat glistened and danced with the breeze, and the emerald-green fields sparkled, the sun continued its journey downwards.

'Have theur still got the cloth you found on the road the other day?' asked John curiously.

'Yea still got it, just in case.'

'I've been thinking about it, we best keep a look out after all,' John urged.

They walked across the dark square and stepped into the Kings Arms. It was packed full of copyholders, freeman, and those wishing to air grievances to the steward. Thomas saw the deputy and his partner standing at the bar talking to the householder. Patrons continued to stream down the stairs into the basement and John, nodding at Thomas, followed.

Ale in hand, they walked down the creeping, rotten wood stairs into the small stone walled room. It brought back bad memories for John, touching his head to feel the scar from the last time he attended the rat baiting.

Thomas thought to himself only the lowest of the local inhabitants with the most vulgar sentimentality would frequent such a place. 'Thy sport attracts the best clientele,' he whispered.

They both scanned the spectators, a loud and angry mob, gesticulating and pointing at what was going on. Then John noticed the two men that had befriended him the previous time. One of them saw him and nodded.

He turned to whisper to Thomas, 'There's that bloke that were here last time. I wonder, not locals and been hangin' about since the trouble started.'

The Steward had travelled to Stanbury for the day to talk to Billy's owner. He passed on the news to his partners that Billy's efforts would not be as significant this night because the owner had not placed the dried herbs in his food. The owner had told him sixteen or seventeen rats.

John made way to a space in the bleachers that climbed up the stone wall. Thomas followed, watching one of the patrons walk past him to the corner of the mud-soaked room to relieve himself. He left a shadow of urine on the wall, then returned, pushing for his place back at the edge of the pit.

Soon after, the rat catcher appeared with his moving hessian bag. He poured the squealing rats into the pit and the crowd cheered. Once again, the champion terrier Billy arrived with his owner. The crowd cheered again.

John and Thomas were more interested in what was going on outside the pit. They watched as the patrons yelled for Billy to take care of business.

The marshal counted, 'Ten… eleven… twelve…' John looked over to see the two men, they were motionless, just watching. *There's something not quite right about those two,* he thought to himself. He tried to remember back to the last time they had met, but it was all too blurry. The last thing he remembered was winning the shillings, then the celebrations, and then nothing. *It was them, but how do I prove it?*

'Fifteen… sixteen… seventeen. Stop!' yelled the marshal, taking the last rat from Billy's quivering jaws, its stomach open, intestines exposed and bloody.

Some of the patrons, angry and confused by the number of rats he had killed, verbally abused the owner and the dog.

John noticed the two men accepting winnings from others, a satisfied look on their faces.

John leant over towards Thomas. 'Those two men they were here last time I was here. I won coin from them,' he said.

Thomas gazed at them. 'They look familiar, I remember them from the manor,' he said. 'They had business with the steward.'

'The steward?' John asked inquisitively.

'Yer, then the steward came over ta William 'n I and gave us an earful,' replied Thomas. 'It was obvious that he was trying to hide something.'

Looking back at the two men, 'There's something not right about those two,' remarked John.

Thomas tried to remember back. 'When I were here that night, they were hanging around you like birds at the first seeding.'

John noticed some of the men going up the stairs. 'Come on, let's get, the court will be starting soon.'

'HERE YEE, HERE YEE, THE HAWORTH MANORIAL COURT IS NOW IN SESSION.

'All who have business on this night come forward and be recognised!' yelled the steward.

Most of the men that were downstairs returned, the room started to fill, and the steward appeared and sat at the end of the table. He announced the names of those paying their fines; the clerk took their coin, the odd chicken or lamb, and made a note in his ledger.

The steward also warned the patrons about the footpads that had robbed unsuspecting citizens on Moorhouse Lane and to steer clear after dark.

'I heard they threatened old Margery Rushworth with a sword 'n attacked young William,' called out one of the patrons.

Another yelled out, 'Catch 'em and put 'em in the rack.'

'Hang the bastards,' said another.

'OFF WITH THEIR HEADS,' another yelled.

'NO, beheadin' is too quick, draw and quarter 'em,' said another from the back of the room.

They were a riley old bunch, but they looked after their own and any outsiders that did the wrong thing would pay for it. This was the way, the way it had been and the way it would be for generations.

The steward rose and lifted his hands to quieten the room, the room hushed. 'GRAND FOLK OF HAWORTH, everything is being done ta find these vermin and rid the nights of danger. The lord has instructed me to put plans in place, and they will be caught 'n punished.'

John and Thomas slowly peered at each other; they were suspicious of the steward.

'Is there any more business? If so, say thy piece now or forever hold thy tongue.' He looked around the room, which remained silent.

The steward continued, 'And we do present and amerce every person who has made a default either in doing fealty or other suit and service which they do owe to this court and the lord of this manor as follows; namely, all gentlemen must pay the sum of five shillings and every other person the sum of two shillings each and do continue all paynes and penalties here to fore be made.'

Men lined up in front of the clerk to pay what they owed. The rabble returned to their arguing, swearing and contempt for the dog that had lost them coin or jubilation and celebration for those who had won.

The Steward ambled over and sat at the card table with the two men Thomas noticed from the manor.

They dealt him in. 'How many?' the steward asked.

'Seventeen,' one of the strangers answered.

'Did you wager it all?' asked the steward picking up another card. His other companion emptied a leather pouch into the middle of the table as if he was making a bet.

The steward placed his ridiculously poor hand on the table face down and picked up all the coin besides four shillings.

The steward stood. 'It's been a pleasure gentleman,' turned and made his way to the door.

'Come Thomas,' said John as he stood up from the bench and approached the two men at the card table.

'John, what are you doing? I have ta be off home,' Thomas said reluctantly.

'Let's see if we can increase thy dowry,' John said, while turning to show Thomas the shillings in his hand.

Thomas rolled his eyes and watched John walk over to the table, pause and sit down on the empty stool with the two strangers. 'Aye up, do you mind if I join you?'

'Of course not, thy coin is as grand as anybody else,' said the stranger, remembering their past interactions.

The other smiled. 'By God you were a state the last time we saw you, we walked part of the way down Sun Street with you then left you to thy own devices.'

'Mmmm, I was going ta ask you about that night, it is such a blur to me.'

Thomas stood afar, took another ale and watched. He wondered how long John's shillings would last, not long after noticing the grimace on his face after the first hand. Thomas expected him to get up so that they could be on their way, but he ordered more ale from the barmaid and continued. Thomas started to lose interest and nod off, he sooo wanted to get back to the cottage but endured. The next time Thomas opened his eyes, he saw John rake the coin from the middle of the table. He could tell that his adversaries were not pleased by the outcome of the hand.

While he dealt, John noticed it, astonished and even a little excited, a small tear not large and mostly hidden by the crimple in the shirt but a tear, with the skin of his forearm noticeable. John wanted to jump up and scream. He looked for the deputy, but most were long gone; what to do, he thought. No need to bring attention to himself. Then he noticed the swords wrapped with a large belt leaning against the wall. *I have to get out of here.*

John held up his hand as one of the other men started to deal the cards. 'Gentlemen, it's getting late 'n it will be an early start. This will be my last hand,' said John, while looking for the whereabouts of Thomas.

'You have won a great deal of our coin again. Will you not allow us ta win some of it back?' enquired one of the men disappointedly.

John looked pleased with himself. 'Another time, I must be off home,' he said while scraping his winnings into his hat and standing to leave.

He turned and walked toward the door, giving Thomas a shake on the shoulder on the way out.

Thomas woke, stunned by the sudden awakening. He looked about then saw John marching toward the door and quickly followed. Through the door they went, passing the night watchman on the way. John was walking at a faster pace than usual.

Thomas quickened his pace and tried to catch up. 'What's wrong John? Why are you in such a hurry?'

'It was them; I saw the tear in his shirt. It was them, the footpads same who walked with me home that night.'

'Joseph and Mary, what are we gonna do?'

'Nowt, don't tell a soul, we'll sleep on it and figure the best way to handle it in the morning.'

By the time Thomas got to the cottage, Margery and William were fast asleep. He could hear Margery's nasal passages vibrating and William was talking in his sleep.

He undressed, leaving his undershirt on and climbed onto the straw-filled mattress, pulling the wool blanket over himself.

The fire was still burning and threw a glow over the room. Thomas would not sleep much that night thinking about what had transpired that evening. He looked for the piece of material in his codpiece, making sure it was still there. He held it, twisting it in his fingers before putting it back, then he picked up the stone that Agnes had given him earlier in the day and he smiled remembering their banter.

John walked back and entered the cottage quietly so as not to wake up Agnes and his wife. Taking out his pipe, he filled it and lit it with a twig from the fire. Sitting there in deep thought for a while, he thought about the two men before undressing and climbing into bed beside his wife. For a while he lay there, eyes open, staring at the shadow dancing on the rafters. He was troubled and knew he wouldn't sleep. He tossed and turned, continually rustling the straw-filled mattress much to Margaret's annoyance.

They were all up before the cock crowed; Agnes dressed quickly and left for the manor, John and Mrs Hargreaves tended to the hide. Later that day, John walked to the manor to see the reeve about what needed to be done on the lord's demesne. He joined Thomas and two others weeding the long strips of wheat that were now waist high. *It wouldn't be long before harvest*, he thought to himself.

'Have you thought about what we're going to do, John? I didn't sleep a wink last night thinkin' about it,' stated Thomas.

John stood up straight to stretch his back. 'You're not a lone traveler there Thomas, I'm gonna speak to the reeve and see what he says.'

After the weeding had been done, they both walked up to the manor. The reeve was outside carrying tools to the barn. Thomas and John followed, bringing the hoes they had used with them.

'Reeve, can we have a word?' called out John as he neared the barn door.

'Words are free,' said the reeve while hanging up the tools.

'We have a matter that requires urgent attention,' called out John.

'The two footpads, we know who they are,' claimed Thomas excitedly.

The reeve turned and walked urgently toward them, he stopped and paused looking past them, considering what to say next. 'Be right careful what you tell me because whatever it be, I must report it to the steward. False accusations could land you in the pillory for slandering.'

Thomas opened his hand, showing the steward the piece of material that he had been holding onto. He went on to explain how he had found it in a patch of bramble where they had been robbed. John then went on to explain how playing cards he had seen a rip in the man's shirt.

'This piece of material could belong ta anybody. It's a bit farfetched, don't you think lads?' the reeve implied.

'I better see the steward, he gets back soon so hold on here.' The reeve walked out of the barn a purpose in his step.

'Christ my Lord, now what are we going to do? I saw the steward with those men. He's involved with them? We'll end up on the pillory for sure, or worse,' Thomas lamented.

A few minutes later the reeve returned. 'His lordship wants ta see thee. Come with me.'

They followed the reeve out of the barn into the daylight; it started to drizzle; they entered the manor through the back door into the kitchen once again. Agnes was there. She looked up surprised to see them. She had a quizzical look on her face while she stood there mixing something in a pot. Thomas raised his eyebrows worriedly but said nothing.

Agnes thought this could only be bad news about the banns. *Has somebody disputed the union and reported to the lord?* She thought the worst.

They entered the great hall. His lordship was sitting at the table the steward had returned and was standing behind him to the left.

Thomas followed John's lead and took off his hat whispering, 'Now we're in for it, we'll be lucky if we don't lose our tongues after all this.'

They walked up to the table nervously.

The lord looked up at them. 'One's reeve tells me that you have news of the footpads that have been working the area?'

John and Thomas paused, looked at each other nervously, neither wanting to say anything, looked at the reeve then back at the lord.

'Goodness me, well speak up man one hasn't got all day. Heavens above! What is good for one's ears is also good for the reeve's.'

Thomas hesitated, 'We know who the footpads are, yer grace.'

Just then, the steward returned and made his way over. 'Reeve have you not work to do outside?'

The reeve bowed, then left.

'Ah steward, I'm glad you have returned, these men have news of the footpads.'

'Have they now?' asked the steward. He stared at them.

'Oh, and how have you come by this information?' enquired the steward.

Thomas excitedly explained how he saw the two strangers in the Kings Arms the night John was robbed and battered, how he had found a piece of cloth on a bramble where the footpads had held them up, and how John had made mention of the rip in the shirt of the two same men that he played cards with.

'It is all linked with the Kings Arms, my Lord,' stated Thomas confidently.

The steward leant down to whisper to his benefactor, 'All hearsay my lord, dismiss it 'n let's get on with other business.'

The lord listened, then paused. 'And what say you, John Hargreaves?'

'My Lord, I admit what young Thomas has said seems farfetched. But I know him as an honest and true man, and I believe what he says deserves further consideration.'

The steward leant down again. 'My Lord, I advise that you dismiss this.'

'Thomas, can you describe these men' asked his lordship.

'Both of 'em wore a black slouch hat. They were not from around 'ere. One had a red sheep skin doublet done up with a whole row of buttons. They had swords and large black belts and were both wearing a tan woolen overcoat.'

'My Lord…' John interrupted, 'My Lord, I believe young Thomas has told all the information that he knows.'

'Let him speak,' commanded the lord.

Thomas paused. 'There is one other thing yer grace; I saw these men accepting coin from the steward at the back of the manor. Thomas looked down at the stone ground, regretting his accusation.

His lordship looked up at the steward, frowning. 'Steward, what do you know of this?'

'May I be excused, your lordship?' The steward dismissed himself and left the great hall. After some minutes, he returned and took his place at the lord's side. He looked at Thomas with disdain.

John whispered, 'Now you've done it.' He imagined a night stuck in the pillory, taking sips of water from the vicar and trying to move his face enough to dodge the rotten potatoes being thrown at him.

'My Lord, somebody is waiting outside that could put an end to this mystery. Would you allow me ta bring them in?' asked the steward mischievously.

Lord Birkhead gestured, and the steward walked toward the big oak door, opening it he allowed the mystery guests to enter.

The two men entered and marched in unison, their hard leather shoes striking the stone floor in unison and causing an echo in the hall. They walked up to the table and stood beside Thomas.

Thomas and John continued to face forward but were shocked when they looked out of the corners of their eyes. *The man with the eye patch.* Thomas wanted to scream and holler but remained silent; John stood there stunned.

The two men bowed and doffed their black slouch hat.

Looking at Thomas and John, the steward said, 'My Lord, may I introduce Joseph Moore and Captain Smythe, formally of the King's Regiment. They are both on thy lordship's purse pursuing the footpads responsible fer recent troubles, not only here in Haworth but also on the road to Stanbury. They have been under my employ for these last weeks.'

'Why wasn't I told about this?' demanded Lord Birkhead.

'My Lord, you commanded me to take care of business in the village. It is right important that the less town folk know the better, lest word gets out. I had instructed them to investigate the Kings Arms, patrol the road to Stanbury and keep watch on Moorhouse Lane.'

The piece of cloth from the shirt. Thomas was still unconvinced. 'My lord, I have a piece of cloth from a shirt we believe belonged to one of the footpads.' He held it up.

'I noticed that the captain has a hole in his shirt,' said John.

The steward frowned, looking suspicious of the two gentlemen in his employ. *Could it have been them all along?*

Captain Smythe took the piece of cloth and looked for the hole, trying to match it. 'You see, it doesn't match. This hole in my garment was caused long ago and I have not had it mended.'

Thomas frowned and looked sadly at John then at his lordship. 'My Lord, if I may, I have done a great disservice to his grace the steward and these gentlemen.'

Lord Birkhead looked up at the steward for guidance, knowing better not to get involved in village matters.

'Calm thyself Thomas Rushworth, now that we know it isn't you two, we can put a plan in place. There will be enough time for the pillory later.'

John looked at Thomas alarmingly.

The lord stood, everybody else bowed as he left the great hall, leaving the steward and his companions. The steward gestured for them to follow him. He walked through another door into a room that was like the last but much smaller. It housed a desk and chair and he asked them to sit at the polished wooden table while he sat behind a sizeable polished oak desk covered in papers and ledgers.

He began to talk of a trap that they would set at a manor court. He asked if John would play the part of the winning drunkard and go home late from the Kings Arms. The steward assured him he and his men would be in constant vigilance and they would follow him. Thomas and William would also accompany him down Moorhouse Lane, but keep themselves hidden by the night. The steward went on to explain how they would allow him to win a large sum at the gaming tables.

As there hadn't been any troubles for a while, they assumed the footpads would strike again soon. The men parted, John and Thomas followed the steward back through the great hall to the kitchen. Agnes looked up worriedly, wandering why they had been in the great hall for so long. She looked at her father and then at Thomas, who winked to belay her worry. They departed the manor and started walking, silent for a lot of the way, no doubt thinking about the events that had transgressed. They parted ways, both intending to work the fields for the rest of the day.

John called out to Thomas, 'Come by tonight to see Agnes if you like,' as he continued toward Marsh Lane.

'Okay John will do, see ya' tonight then.'

Thomas walked through the wheat fields. It was over waist height now and soon, at the height of summer, they would harvest. It was hard back-breaking work, but it was also a time to celebrate; it was time to sharpen the scythe, he thought.

CHAPTER 15

THE ANGEL

As Thomas neared home, he could see William chopping wood in the distance. The dogs could smell his scent and came bounding through the wheat to greet him. William threw his last split log on the pile and turned. He wiped the sweat from his brow and lifted his hand to shade his eyes from the sun to see what the dogs were up to. Thomas bent down to pat the dogs, tails wagging. He picked up a small stick and threw it. They bounded after it, black lips flapping and drool coming out the side of their mouth and trailing behind them. They both reached the stick at the same time, picking it up, growling and trying to wrestle it away. Both attempting to be the one to drop it at Thomas' feet.

Thomas paused, he pulled a spike of wheat from the stem of a plant, rubbed it between his hands to test its maturity. He placed some of the grain on his tongue then chewed it to see if it cracked. It didn't. A few more days, he thought to himself.

When Thomas got home, he took the stone out that Agnes had given him to throw at the branch in the vegetable garden. Standing at the grinding wheel, he turned the handle and started to cut and smooth it, reducing the rough edges and shaping it. He dipped the stone into the water bucket and marveled at the stone's colour which started to reveal itself. After he had ground it down to a reasonable size, he walked to the beck and the dogs followed.

Play biting and drooling, they tried to dominate each other with their huge paws by jumping up and placing them on each other's back, the submissive one laying down on her back, extending her legs defensively. The other big male, leaving her to bound ahead to catch up to Thomas, who paid no attention to their games. The bitch, feeling left behind, pulled herself up, grumbled and took off after them.

Thomas used the sand and gravel and started to polish the stone until the quartz shimmered. He continued to work the stone, his hands becoming stained from the iron oxide. Once finished, Thomas held the stone in his hand, moving it back and forth so that it caught the light. The afternoon was getting on, so he put the stone away and started walking back to the cottage.

'Ya orl right, brother?' asked William.

Thomas began to tell William what had happened at the manor and the plans they had made with the steward.

'That's right dangerous Thomas!' exclaimed William.

Thomas put on a brave face. 'Yea, but what else are we to do when the steward asks? And besides, John has already agreed, and I'll not leave him to his fate alone.'

'You best not tell mother because she'll be worried sick. What if something were to happen? I'm comin' with thee.'

'You are not William, you'll stay here and look after mother!'

'Thomas if anything happened to you mother would never forgive me. I'm comin' with ya', and there's nowt ya' can do about it.'

'You're stubborn.' Thomas knew it was no use continuing once William had made up his mind about something.

'Yer and you know where we both get that from,' replied William, grinning as they both turned to see Margery coming out of the door with the yoke and water buckets to take to the beck.

'Thomas, William, don't you two be too long dawdling, there's work to be done.' Margery looked at Thomas. 'Ya 'orl right son?'

'Aye mother, just been to the beck.' He walked toward her.

'Been ta the beck? Should 'a taken the buckets with thee, save me a walk in the mornin'.'

'Mother I had other things on my mind, want ta see?'

Thomas brought out a piece of cloth and opened it carefully so Margery could see it.

Margery looked down, and as Thomas opened the rag she was taken aback by the beauty of the stone. It shimmered; the quartz sparkled in the dimming light.

'Thomas, that is right beautiful, Agnes will love it.'

'Aye, has sentimental value, not that she knows about it yet.'

'You're a good lad Thomas, Agnes is a lucky lass. I know I don't say it much, but your father would be very proud of you.'

Thomas looked down sadly. He didn't think much about his father these days but felt a warmness when he did. He folded the cloth back up and placed it back in his codpiece for safe keeping.

At the end of the day, Thomas walked to Moorhouse Lane. 'Ayeup, anybody at home? It's Thomas.'

'Come in, Thomas,' called out John. 'Just got back me self, how was yer day?'

Thomas looked weary. 'Long and hard. It's hard enough working for your own, even harder labourin' for somebody else's dinner.'

'Aye that, but there's worse off than we.' John thinking of the Recusant Catholics being rounded up and tortured in York and London. Thomas sat down at the table opposite John.

Mrs Hargreaves poured an ale and put a bowl of pottage in front of them. 'There ya' are, get that into ya' there's fresh veg and a slice of meat.'

Thomas wanted to discuss the coming events of the day but thought better of it with Mrs Hargreaves present.

Agnes walked through the door and was pleasantly surprised to see Thomas; she smiled as she closed the door behind her. Agnes was a little puffed from the walk home and her cheeks were rosy from the night air.

'Would ya' like some supper daughter?' Mrs Hargreaves poured and offered her a jack of ale.

'The ales fine ma, we shared the leftovers from the lord's dinner. His dog was too full of lunch. Must be the best-fed dog in the parish, feed a family of seven with what he throws to that hound,' uttered Agnes.

Thomas grinned, 'Aye, best I grow ears and a tail.'

They all laughed, appreciating that Thomas was starting to feel more comfortable around them.

'Agnes bring Thomas' mattress over here and put it near the fire. You can sleep here tonight. Agnes, there's clean water and a brush if ya' want to get ready for bed? It's been a long day.'

Agnes disappeared to the back of the cottage while Thomas stood and took the mattress from her.

Once again, Mrs Hargreaves put a linen sheet on the mattress and started sewing. Thomas got undressed down to his undershirt.

When Agnes returned, she was dressed in her nightshirt, and she laid down beside him.

He said nothing but had a disgruntled look on his face as he stared up at the thatch.

Agnes giggled seeing him there in the light of the fire, bundled up again.

'Not again,' he whispered to himself.

Agnes giggled again and touched his hand reassuringly, then turned over to go to sleep.

Thomas' mind was too active, and he couldn't sleep, still excited from the events of the day.

It seemed like Thomas had only just fallen asleep when the cock crowed. He turned to see Agnes, but she had already dressed and made her way to the manor.

'Could somebody please get me out of this thing?'

'Okay, 'old on ta ya' horses.' Mrs Hargreaves took a knife and cut Thomas free.

He stood, dressed, and ran out the door after Agnes before Mrs Hargreaves could even offer breakfast. She shook her head in frustration.

He could see her torch making way to Sun Street. He ran faster and called out to her. 'Agnes!' he yelled.

He saw the torch stop. She waited for him.

'Thomas, what are ya' doin'? You'll make me late for the kitchen.'

Thomas slowed as he neared her. He bent over, put his hands on his knees trying to catch his breath.

'Ya' all right, Thomas?' she asked, smiling at his enthusiasm.

He continued to gasp, stood placing his hands on his hips, leaning back. 'Agnes,' he paused and continued to breathe heavily. He took the stone that he had cut and polished out of his codpiece, knelt on one knee. 'Agnes, I would be honoured if you would wed me.'

Agnes smiled. 'I thought that was already a bygone conclusion.'

'Aye, a conclusion decided by the church and by our parents, not by you.' He looked up at her, holding the rock between his fingers.

She took it and looked closer to see the quartz sparkling in the light of the torch. 'Is this the rock from our wager?'

'Yes.' Thomas smiled.

'Thomas, I don't know what to say,' she paused. 'Nobody has ever… It's beautiful.' She looked into his eyes.

He stood looking at her while she continued to move the stone back and forth between her fingers. Looking up at him she smiled. 'Thomas, I don't know what ta' say, 'tis the most beautiful thing I've ever seen.'

Agnes held it tightly in her hand, stood on her tiptoes and gently caressed his face. She brought his face down to hers. He closed his eyes waiting for their lips to touch, lingering for just a moment.

She turned and continued walking up the hill toward the manor.

Stopping halfway up the hill, she turned. 'It has been a pleasure spending time with you this morning Thomas Rushworth, I hope we might do it again sometime.'

He opened one eye to see Agnes standing up the hill in front of him. He smiled and turned toward home then realised, 'AGNES YA' DIDN'T GIVE ME YER ANSWER!'

She didn't answer. Agnes kept walking, forcing herself not to look back.

'Yes,' she said quietly, still not looking back.

'WHAT, I DIDN'T HEAR YA'?' said Thomas, taking three steps forward inquisitively.

'THOMAS YER GONNA WAKE THE DEAD, SHUUSH!' Agnes continued to walk up the hill, she didn't look back and raised her voice just a little, 'YEEEES!'

Thomas, hands on hips, looked down at the ground. He could hear her saying something, he took another two steps forward.

'AGNEEEES,' he yelled.

Agnes stopped and turned; Thomas could see her. She looked like an angel, the torch like a beacon, illuminated her. Stars from the heavens twinkled brightly behind her.

'YES, Thomas Rushworth, I will WED YOU!' She turned toward the manor and ran.

The dogs started barking, neighbours who were waking called out in anger. Thomas stood there for a moment in the dark, watching the torch until it disappeared over the hill. The cottagers started to stoke their fires, light their candles and fill their oil lamps. Doors opened, shutters slammed, but it was still too dark for them to see him. He turned and headed for home.

The cook heard her approach and walked to the corner to pick up the whipping stick. As Agnes opened the door, he grabbed her by the arm, swung her around and lashed her on the buttocks six times.

'I'VE TOLD YOU ABOUT BEIN' LATE! Don't be late again, get ta ya' duties,' he walked up and put the stick back in the corner and continued cracking the eggs.

Agnes grimaced and rubbed her bottom, walked to the pantry and picked up the apples and started peeling them for the lord's apple pie. She had done it so many times that she didn't have to look, preferring to think about other things.

CHAPTER 16

HARVEST OF LIFE

Later, further down the hill, Thomas and William walked along the furrows, picking weeds and checking for pests.

It was boring, monotonous work, but they knew what the yields would bring; flour for bread and biscuits and enough grain to pay the lord and barter for other food and provisions. Life was a circle, harvest, rain, drought, seed, harvest, rain, drought and harvest.

With the harvest so close there was jubilation and joy, an excitement in the village. Shopkeepers and merchants knew that after the harvest trade would improve. It was a time of excitement, like a heavy rain after a drought.

John had agreed to help and other neighbours were ready to lend a hand. On a good day, they could reap an acre to an acre and a half in a day. Then, of course, there was the lord's demesne, where all tenants would work together to harvest his wheat.

The wheat was golden and almost shoulder height. Thomas and William had sharpened the scythes, and they had been lucky with the rains holding off lest it ruin the crop. A few drops the previous night, but today the sky was a bright blue. Many were on hand and John, Mrs Hargreaves and Agnes had come up to the hide to lend a hand. The steward always provided time away from the manor during the harvest.

John, William and Thomas were the reapers and began to swing the scythe and cut the wheat. The wheat was caught in a cradle on the scythe and fell onto the ground to their left in a neat and square line. They aimed to have the swath cut the same length so that they would be bundled more easily. When harvesting, it was important to keep the scythe close to the ground to maximise the length of the cut and to preserve what was left in the ground. The stubble needed to be as short as possible; however, hitting the ground with the scythe meant it would need re-sharpening.

On the odd occasion, you could hear the exclamation of one of the men who had done just that. The men were proficient and usually could go a good thirty yards before the scythe required re-sharpening.

Following on behind were Margery, Agnes and children from the village, the gatherers, who made a band out of stems to tie up the wheat. The swath was then laid on the band ready for the bandster to tie the swath up and for the other two bandsters to stack the completed sheaf with others creating a stook. The stook stood upright and was then left to cure and dry for a couple of days before being loaded onto a cart and taken away for threshing and winnowing to separate the wheat from the stalks.

Finally came Mrs Hargreaves and Cousin Mary, the rakers who, with a specially designed stubble rake, cleared the ground of any loose stalks of wheat ready for them to be banded up lest waste anything that good God had provided them. They were placed near the stook but were treated differently in the threshing process as they could contain dirt and stones picked up during the raking process. Often the women folk would keep this and grind it themselves.

The sun was high, and it was hot back breaking work. Margery had placed a tankard of ale under a nearby tree and both she and Mrs Hargreaves had brought cheese and bread to eat at mid-day. Occasionally, Thomas would look up to see Agnes bent over tying bands around the swath. *She's a hard worker*, he thought to himself. On one occasion, she looked up and their eyes met. They smiled at each other without saying a word and continued to the task at hand.

At midday they all gathered in the shade under a tree in the middle of the field, the one not chopped down for just that purpose. Dark, sweaty patches grew under the arms of the men and their backs were sodden with sweat. Agnes pulled the pieces of straw from the bottom of her kirtle, then helped Mrs Hargreaves pour ale from the jug to share. Bread and cheese were broken and passed around the men, the women taking their share afterwards.

'This is a good start,' exclaimed Thomas, relishing the shade as he sat using the trunk of the tree to support his back.

'Aye, but many acres to go. I'll bring my ox and cart tomorra' and we can start loading it up to take back to yours for threshing,' stated John.

Margery, with Mrs Hargreaves and Agnes' help, would be responsible for thrashing the long stalks on the ground separating the grain. They would then rake away the debris and finally flip the grain with a shovel, allowing the lightweight waste particles to be carried away by the wind. The grain would then be left to dry in the sun for a couple of days to reduce the moisture content. Finally, they would shovel it into bags to be taken to the manor for milling.

They were forced to take their harvest to the lord's manor, where the bags would be counted, and he would take his ten percent. Here the grain would be milled, turned into flour and re-bagged. It was a long, tedious process, but one that would see them through the winter and beyond until the next harvest, God willing.

It would take them over a month to harvest their hide, the lord's demesne and any neighbour's hide's that were caught behind. If there was the smell of rain in the air, then it would be all hands to the fields, and they would harvest through the night if needed. The finish of harvest was a time to celebrate and socialise with others in the same situation. It was also an appropriate time for a handfasting.

CHAPTER 17

FIRST WOMAN

After the sermon, the vicar coughed and read out the announcements from the pulpit. 'By the power of our Lord Jesus Christ, our saviour, and our sovereign King James the first of England and Scotland, I herewith announce the banns of marriage between Thomas Rushworth, son of Thomas and Margery, of Haworth, and Agnes Hargreaves, daughter of John and Margaret of Oxenhope. This is the third time of asking, if any of you know cause or just impediment why these two persons should not be joined together in Holy Matrimony, ye are to declare it.' The vicar announced that the handfasting would take place after prayers the following Sunday and that it would take place at the door of the church because it was the most public place in the village and all that gathered could witness it. Thomas and Agnes touched hands discretely and looked at each other, void of any public display of sentiment.

'Now let us pray.'

'Lord, the source of all true love, we pray for this couple. Grant to them joy of heart, seriousness of mind and reverence of spirit, that as they enter the oneness of marriage, they may be strengthened and guided by you, through Jesus Christ our Lord. Amen.'

'Amen', the congregation repeated in unison.

'Lord of love, we pray for Thomas and Agnes. be with them in all their preparations and on their wedding day. Give them your love

in their hearts throughout their married life together, through Jesus Christ our Lord. Amen.'

'Amen.'

⁂

The day had finally arrived. It was an affair with the immediate families, neighbours, friends and anybody else from the parish that happened by to ensure witnesses. It took place at the door of the Church of Saint Michaels All Angels. Agnes and Thomas stood facing each other. Beside Agnes stood William the protector, who took his responsibilities as best man very seriously. Standing behind were John and Mrs Hargreaves, who was wiping a tear from her eye with a linen cloth. They both wore their Sunday best, which they had replaced for the occasion. A new wimple and ochre-coloured gown for Mrs Hargreaves and new hose and a brand-new red tunic for Mr Hargreaves.

Agnes wore a chaplet of lilies in her hair, and a green gown that settled on the tops of her soft slippers. Her hair was long, and she had washed it in the beck. It shone in the sunlight. She had pinched her cheeks to make them rosy and rubbed her lips with a blackberry.

Thomas had removed his hat and wet his hair, ensuring that the cowlick on the crown of his head behaved itself. He had shaved with the blade, being careful not to cut the skin, especially in that soft part just below the chin. He had donned his Sunday best hose and washed the foot coverings in the beck, allowing them to dry in the sun. When he saw her, the flowers in her hair, he smiled. She smiled back confidently. He looked at John, who looked prim and proper in his new tunic.

John gave him a wink of encouragement, so proud he was of his daughter and their new son; he coughed to fight back the lump that was slowly growing in his throat. The vicar raised his clenched fist to his mouth, quietly coughed, then commenced.

'The grace of our Lord Jesus Christ, the love of God, and the fellowship

of the Holy Spirit be with you. God is love, and those who live in love live in God and God lives in them.'

'In the presence of God, Father, Son and Holy Spirit, we have come together to witness the marriage of Agnes and Thomas, to pray for God's blessing on them, to share their joy and to celebrate their love. In good times and in bad, may find strength, companionship and comfort, and grow to maturity in love. Marriage is a way of life made holy by God and blessed by the presence of our Lord Jesus Christ with those celebrating a wedding at Cana in Galilee.'

The vicar paused. 'First, I am required to ask anyone present who knows a reason why this man and this woman may not marry, to declare it now.'

The vicar then took their opposite hands and placed them together, then wrapped a scarf around their wrists as a sign of commitment.

'Thomas, will you take Agnes to be your wife? Will you love her, comfort her, honour and protect her, and, forsaking all others, be faithful to her as long as you both shall live?'

'I will,' Thomas smiled nervously.

Agnes looked up at Thomas. 'Agnes, will you take Thomas to be your husband? Will you love him, comfort him, honour and protect him, and, forsaking all others, be faithful to him as long as you both shall live?'

'I will,' said Agnes.

'In the presence of God, and before this congregation, Agnes and Thomas have given their consent and made their marriage vows to each other. They have declared their marriage by the joining of hands and by the giving and receiving of gifts. I, therefore, proclaim that they are husband and wife.'

The onlookers cheered, then walked into the main building of the church for traditional prayers and of course the vicar's sermon, which involved blessings for the happy couple and sermon on the sanctity of marriage.

After prayers, they all returned to the village green and most of the congregation followed, including neighbours, friends and anybody else that was around and assured of free drink and ale. Most of them had brought food or gifts for the bride and groom. There was a chicken locked in a wooden cage who, unused to the confinement continually squawked and pecked to get out. There was a small roll of linen, various bags of vegetables, carved wooden bowls and other items that would help the couple to start married life. Three large tables had been set up, placed end to end and covered with clean white linen tablecloths. Margery, Mrs Hargreaves, and Cousin Mary poured the bride-ale, a special batch for the celebration made with extra malt, into clay tankards and placed them along the table. Each time a guest refilled his tankard he would place a coin on the table which would be collected later and given to the bride to commence housekeeping.

A lamb had been slaughtered and was currently roasting on a spit. Two young men carried the top of a table holding numerous bowls of potato and onion soup, which guests eagerly took.

Three musicians sat on stools, one with a pear-shaped lute, the other with a bagpipe, and the third with a tabor snare drum. They played a joyful, lively jig as four guests stood near the table holding hands and dancing to the triple time rhythm.

Thomas and Agnes sat on a bench at the middle table, not saying much but watching and smiling as the children raced to and fro barefoot, squealing and giggling when caught.

Behind them was a portrait painted by nature, green valley and dale, undulating hills speckled with woolly white. The manor sitting there in all its glory, a beacon of power among the strips and squares of the countryside. Beyond, the wildness of the moors which touched the deep blue, clear sky in the distance. The valley gently sloped to the beck in the background, which was lined with oak, lime, and beech trees. The roughness of the banks lacked the cultivations of the tilled land and the brownness contrasted the deep greens. The dark brown line of the lane snaked its way up and then east toward the horizon.

William sat away from Agnes, dispensing with his protection responsibilities for a time, so he could slurp his potato and onion soup and salivate at the smell of the lamb being turned on the spit. John sat beside Thomas and was already into his third tankard of strong ale.

The two dogs sat in front of the spit, drooling and watching the oil drip slowly from the roasting lamb into the fire. Their eyes recovering to watch the next drip as it collected on the bottom of the roast and start its downward journey once again.

Then, it was time for the running for the bride's door. Thomas, William and the other men from the village lined up in front of a rope that John had unraveled and laid out along the green, green grass of home. Agnes stood at the side, lifted her hand with a handkerchief that Thomas had given her for a wedding gift. Eagerly, the men crouched, ready to run. They would run as fast as they could to the bride's cottage, using any means possible to thwart the others.

As Agnes lifted the handkerchief, the men readied for the signal and quietened their banter, all except Thomas and William who carried on while standing next to each other in the line-up.

William whispered, 'Brother you best not run, I don't want ya' to embarrass yourself in front of yer' new wife.'

'Don't you worry 'bout me, I'll be taking my first sip of the ale before you knock on the door,' Thomas whispered.

'Save your energy for the night brother, you may need it.'

'Fear not William, I've enough energy to run past you and still have some for the obligations.'

The crowd hushed and as Agnes dropped the handkerchief they cheered excitedly. The men took off across the field, pushing and jostling in the process until they got clear. William had got the start on Thomas, but he grabbed the back of his tunic and pulled him backwards. William lost his balance but managed to keep himself upright and trailed Thomas by a small margin. Thomas was slowly catching up to the two leaders, five paces in front, who were jostling and elbowing each other for the lead. One of them flung out his elbow and hit the other in the chest, which allowed him to get out in front.

The second runner, slightly winded, slowed a little. 'Bastard!' he yelled angrily. He recovered and paced himself just behind the leader.

Thomas was only two paces behind him now and William a further two paces behind Thomas. The two men slowed as they neared the dry-stone wall to climb over it, but Thomas kept his speed and hurled himself over it at full pace, remembering the races that he and William had as young boys. William did the same and overtook the two men who were arguing and swearing at each other in frustration, as they saw the two brothers gain a lead as they ran up the unploughed field. They took off after them, but both William and Thomas had a good lead now. Thomas didn't look back but could hear and feel William gaining on him. They were only one hundred paces from the cottage now, and Thomas and William were breathing heavily, sweat beading and dripping from their faces. They knew the lay of the land, having run it often as children. The others didn't and struggled with the steepness of the climb.

William caught up to Thomas and ran stride for stride. 'GIVE UP BROTHER YER RACE IS OVER,' he called out with laboured breath.

They were only fifty paces from the cottage now, and they could both sense victory.

'NOT YET IT ISN'T!' yelled Thomas. 'YOU CLAIM VICTORY TOO EARLY.'

Twenty paces, Thomas could feel his speed slowing and was fearful, as the younger William was starting to get a slight lead. Thomas tried to draw every ounce of speed that he had to keep up to him, then while level he barged into William with his shoulder, knocking him off balance.

William gained his balance. 'SARD,' but slowed and watched as Thomas ran up to the door.

Thomas looked behind and lifted the latch to the cottage. Once inside, panting heavily, he put his hands on his knees and tried to recoup his breath. William stood at the door doing the same, neither able to speak.

Still finding it difficult, William, still panting, forced a sentence 'Yer' a cheatin' rogue brother.' He took a deep breath and walked inside.

The house had been fully cleaned; the shutters were open, and dust particles glistened in the sunlight as it angled down to the floor. The earthen floor had been swept and new, fresh straw had been scattered over it. A bed had been placed downstairs with a fine linen curtain around it. There were freshly cleaned bed coverings near the fire. Decorative flowers had been placed to add colour to the usually drab walls. Rose petals had been placed on the bed and water buckets were full of fresh water from the beck. A bowl of apples had been placed on the table on the other side of the fire, no doubt from the lord's orchard, with the reeve's permission. A linen sheet had been hung from the ceiling to cover the animal's quarters, which had been shoveled out and replaced with straw and new hay, which had the musty fragrance of a spring day after rain.

Thomas, slowly getting his breath back, walked to the bed pulled down the blanket to reveal the pewter tankard filled with warm ale. He carefully picked it up and took a sip, then offered it to William.

'No brother tis yours... enjoy and I hope you choke on it,' William claimed sarcastically. He smiled.

Thomas took a deep breath, smiled, and took another swig while he walked to the door. 'Come on William, we must be getting back.' They both walked out the door, William shutting it behind him.

Halfway between the cottage and the dry-stone wall they could see the other two competitors squaring up to fight, each had their fists clenched and raised threateningly. Circling each other to try and find an opening for the first punch to be thrown. Thomas and William walked past them and said nothing, letting them get on with it.

Arriving back at the village green, the guests were all full of joy and celebration, and they cheered as they saw Thomas and William approach with their arms around each other's shoulders.

Agnes stood to see what they were cheering at. She saw Thomas walking across the green and was quietly excited when she saw him carefully carrying the pewter tankard. He drew closer, and she walked out to stand in front of the table. He walked up and knelt on one knee, holding the tankard up to her. She accepted it and the guests all cheered. She drank what was left, then gave it back to him as a gift to be treasured. Agnes then reached under her gown, pulling a small red ribbon that was tied to her upper leg. She handed it to Thomas and lightly kissed him on the cheek, the guests cheered again.

'Well done 'usband, seems like you have hidden talents.'

'No wife, I am humbled by my brother's grace, for it was he that should have won, and my love for you forced me to be a lesser man under the circumstances.'

'Quiet yourself husband, for I know of your brother's love for you and your love for him. He would not claim any misfortune attributed to you.'

John by this time had consumed his fair share of the bride-ale and was destined for the ale passion the following morning.

The musicians continued to play; the guests continued to dance. Two men, holding one of their hands aloft and a tankard in the other, danced a colourful jig. It involved a complicated series of foot touching to the beat of the tabor snare drum. Margery and Mrs Hargreaves, busy filling tankards, stopped for a minute and clapped in time to the rhythm. The beat got quicker and quicker until the men couldn't keep up and fell in a heap on the ground to the amusement of everybody else who laughed at their expense.

Thomas and Agnes smiled as they gazed at John looking a touch tipsy from the bride-ale, a small mound of coin gradually growing before him. He placed another penny on the pile and refilled his tankard.

'Ya' 'orl right there John?' asked Thomas, smiling.

'Orl' right? Neverrrr beeeeen better,' he slurred his speech and tried to stand but thought ill of it and sat back down again.

Four men at the furthest end of the table started muggling, a drinking game to see who sculled the most bride-ale. The first man sculled a jack of ale, the second man two, the third three, the fourth four, and then the first man began again with five. John Hargreaves began with six, much to his wife's disgust as she rolled her eyes. She said nothing.

The game would continue through the night or, for as long as they could remain upright.

The sun was starting to set, the musicians were out of tune or quiet, and the dancers had stopped dancing. All but one lone chap who continued a slow jig by candlelight, still hearing the imaginary music of the day.

Margery, Cousin Mary and Mrs Hargreaves finally got a chance to wind down, take what was left of the bride-ale and cut off a taste of the remnants of the cold lamb that had stopped turning.

Mrs Hargreaves took a sip of the ale. 'Ohh, Mrs Rushworth, that's a fine drop. I can taste the extra malt and the love you put into it, must have taken a season to brew that.'

'Mrs Hargreaves, I started brewing it the first time I saw you and Agnes in the village market that day.' She winked.

She thought back to that morning in the village square, a misty morning with the clouds being stubborn to make way for the sun. Stalls set in rows with each cottager tabling their wares from fruit to fry. Linen wimples, trinkets and carvings, all seen before. Margery looked through one stall to another and briefly saw a young woman, following her mother, such bearing and posture, unspoilt, a Yorkshire beauty, but she didn't know it.

Mrs Hargreaves laughed, a deep belly laugh, leaning back raising her eyes in the direction of the stars. 'Mrs Rushworth please, you are dear to me, please... Call me Margaret.'

'Aye, Margaret, has a nice sound to it.' Margery smiled in acceptance and gratitude for her approval and friendship.

Mrs Hargreaves thought back to when they had first met and the support and friendship she had offered a family of Recusant Catholics.

Agnes, seeing them together was warmed by their friendship.

'Mother, Mrs Rushworth, Cousin Mary, thank you so much for making this such a special day.'

'Agnes, I think that's a bit formal. From here on in, please call me Margery... or Mother.'

Agnes walked up to Margery, putting her arms around her and looking in her eyes, she whispered, 'Thank-you, Mother.'

Turning around, she noticed that her own mother had a tear in her eye and was looking away, wiping it away with one finger discretely.

She walked up to her mother and stopped in front of her. Mrs Hargreaves, at first looking away, composed herself, then turned to look at her daughter straight in the eyes.

She looked down and held her hands; she started to caress the backs of them with her thumb, slowly at first, then squeezed them lightly.

'Agnes, you are the world to me.' She held back the tears. 'I love you so much and wish you so much happiness and love.'

Agnes started to tear but held it back until she threw her arms around her neck and then her eyes began to water. 'Don't mother, or else I'll be a blubbering mess on my wedding night.'

Most had left the common green, but those that stayed accompanied Agnes and Thomas to the threshold of the door to their cottage.

The vicar unlatched the front door and went in, flicking holy water in front of him. He arrived in front of the bed and flicked holy water in the sign of the cross. Thomas lifted Agnes and carried her across the threshold to ensure that she didn't look too eager to consummate the marriage. Cousin Mary, William, Mrs Hargreaves, Margery and several neighbours followed them inside. As Thomas and Agnes prepared themselves for bed, the visitors opened the fine linen curtains around the bed and pulled down the blankets and lit candles.

The happy couple appeared from different corners of the room, both disrobed to their undershirts. They climbed into bed and the linen curtains were pulled back around. Nothing was said, then everybody left except Cousin Mary, the last to leave. She pulled the door behind her, ensuring the latch was in place, but stood outside the door.

The neighbours departed, William went back to the common green to help John to his feet, who by this time was in no condition to walk unaided. Margery lit a torch and they all started walking toward the Hargreaves cottage where they would spend the night.

In the cottage, Agnes and Thomas shyly continued to stare up at the rafters. Agnes reached over and touched Thomas' hand like she used to do when he was bundled. This time he reciprocated and held her hand, caressing it with his fingers. Saying nothing, they both turned to stare into each other's eyes.

'I still haven't collected from our wager,' whispered Thomas.

'Well, you better be quick about it,' she smiled, turned on her side and leant closer to him.

Thomas put his hand on the side of her face gently; she placed hers on his. He thought about the past weeks and the fondness and growing love that he had for her. He leant closer, closed his eyes and kissed her on the lips. Her hair cascaded over his face as he did. She obliged and moved her face, keeping her lips pressed against his. She felt a closeness to him and felt emotionally safe. They parted lips.

'Oh Thomas, I'm so happy,' she reached down and lifted her undershirt over her head.

Thomas did likewise. He lifted himself on his elbow to face her; she turned on her back, and he kissed her again. He could feel one of her breasts touching his chest and this aroused him. She could feel a stiffness on her leg and shifted over so that he was directly on top of her. He lifted himself slightly from elbows to hands and caressed her hair, moving it from her forehead with his finger. She smiled. He reminded himself of how much she meant to him and how she had become a part of his life. They kissed again, this time she lifted her knees and opened them so that he could lie between them. 'Ohh Thomas.'

She lifted her hands and stroked his arms, looking up at him with come to me eyes. Her hair framed her face, and her expression was relaxed and inviting. He tried to guide himself into the wetness that he could feel. She guided it and took a breath, feeling an intimacy that she hadn't felt before. She put her hands on the small of his back and pulled him closer to her. She gasped and tilted her head backwards. He could feel a tightness, but it was warm and comforting. She pushed his hips away from her; he obliged and then she pulled him close once more, she gasped again and groaned. The tightness that he felt started to subside and it felt deeper. Thomas raised his hips back and pushed down harder and faster, raised them again. Agnes closed her eyes and tilted her head back once more, holding onto his arms tightly. Her breathing started to quicken, Thomas reacted and continued to thrust. Agnes grabbed his buttocks again, this time widening her legs so that he could come closer to her.

Cousin Mary, who had her ear pressed to the door, as was the custom, smiled, turned and walked away toward Moorhouse Lane.

Thomas and Agnes looked up at the rafters, both panting. Agnes turned over and rested on her elbows, her hair fell to the pillow hiding her face. She gave Thomas a small kiss on his chest, looking down at him lovingly and silently playing with the chest hair. Thomas just laid there, trying to catch his breath and gather his thoughts about what had just occurred. He had never felt such a way before. He felt brave, inspired and complete.

Agnes pushed the blanket off, rolled over and stood up. Thomas watched her. She stood there to reveal herself to him. Thomas was awestruck and reluctant to look at anything but her face, but he glimpsed at her breasts but refused to stare directly at them. He could see them through her cascading brown hair, they were pert and perfectly shaped, the nipples erect and dark. She kneeled on the bed, smiled and gave Thomas a small peck on the lips. Not expecting it, he was late to respond.

Feeling more confident, he sat up and looked through the curtain for her. He folded his undershirt and placed it on the bottom of the bed as his mother had taught him. He felt a wetness on his leg, so he moved the blanket to reveal a bloodied patch. He stood and checked himself in the glow of the fire.

'SARD.' He stood up quickly from the bed, worriedly calling out, 'AGNES, AGNES?'

Excitedly, Agnes came running. 'Thomas, what's wrong?'

'THERE'S BLOOD!'

'Calm thyself 'usband, all is well, 'tis the mark of a married woman, do not fear.' She walked through the curtain, smiled and placed a woolen cover on the mattress before climbing back under the blanket. She looked up to see Thomas' nakedness.

He had broad shoulders and muscular arms; she followed the contour of his body down from his chest along the drip of dark hair which leeched from his belly button to his manhood. She blushed when he noticed her looking, then, realising what she was looking at, he jumped quickly back into bed. He cried out in pain as his tailbone cracked the wooden base, the straw having moved and flattened in the process of their lovemaking.

Agnes frowned. 'Thomas, y'orl right? 'usband are ya' hurt?' He laid back smiled as did she, then she giggled.

Thomas cracked a cheeky smile. 'Wife, d'ya think it's funny? I'll show ya' what's funny,' he proceeded to tickle her at the sides of her naked waist.

She laughed briefly, then her face turned serious. 'No Thomas, please don't do it, I hate it!'

Thomas stopped immediately. They both laid down. 'I was worried about ya', seeing the blood.'

'No need. I'm surprised you don't know the ways of a woman.'

'Well, it never came up and then da passed and I suppose ma was well, too shy ta speak of it. I've seen the lambs bein' born.'

'Ahaha Thomas, it's a little different.' Agnes lifted his arm and put it around her neck, using it to snuggle into his chest. She adored his innocence.

She had seen her mother doing a similar thing to her father many times in the dim light of the fire while she pretended to be asleep. She remembered hearing her mother trying to be quiet as her father climbed on top of her and started; first she would gasp, then remain quiet until he finished. He would roll over and start snoring and she could sense her mother lying there with her eyes open, looking up at the darkness. She prayed that she and Thomas would never be so methodical.

She gently rubbed the hairs on his stomach with the tips of her fingers, then moved them up to his chest. This started to arouse him again and she could see the growing mound raising the blanket below. He turned and maneuvered himself between her legs once again. This time he needed no guidance. They would engage in their love making two more times that night and fall asleep exhausted from the day and the exertions of the night.

As the cock crowed, they stirred. The fire had burnt down to an ember, the tallow candles had dripped their waxy design, and the two apple cores on the table beside the bed had browned.

Agnes sat on the edge of the bed then stood. She walked through the thin linen curtain. Thomas feigned being asleep and watched her walk away. He said nothing but was intrigued by her nakedness. Her waist was slim, and her buttocks were round and taught. Her hair tumbled and curled on her back. She had long slender legs and she walked on her tiptoes, which made calves pronounced. Looking closer, he noticed the red welts on her buttocks and upper thighs.

She walked to the freshwater bucket and washed herself, but it stung. She brushed her hair and dressed quickly. Trying to raise the flame in the fire and failing that, placed more kindling and blew so that it caught onto the new dried twigs. The fire grew as she placed a log, and she could hear the pottage in the cauldron start to bubble. She looked back at Thomas; he hadn't moved, still laying there with his chest exposed and his arms raised above his head. His hair was a muddled mess, a bearded shadow darkened his chin, but there was a calmed, satisfied expression on his face.

Agnes lifted the curtains and walked through. She knelt on the bed, leaned down and kissed his forehead. She whispered, 'I'm going to love you forever, Thomas Rushworth.'

Agnes, already late, lifted the latch, looked back one more time and closed the door behind her.

The cook heard her approach and walked to the corner to pick up the whipping stick. As Agnes opened the door, he grabbed her by the arm, swung her around.

'PLEASE, please no more, I'M SORRY!'

He lashed her on the back of the legs while Johnny Nutter the baker watched. 'COOK! That's enough, she got married yesterday.'

The other kitchen maids clapped and cheered, then lined up to hug her lovingly. The cook clapped his hands together. 'Right. Enough of that, back ta mixin' and doin.' The cook looked at Agnes with a stern face. 'Don't be late again, get ta' ya' mixin'.'

Agnes drew a breath, she tried to smile and ignore the stinging pain. She walked to the pantry, chose the ingredients for the lord's spiced porridge and started to mix. She still felt dazed from lack of sleep but accepted the tiredness as a reminder of the night before.

CHAPTER 18

THE ABSENT PREDATOR

'Are you ready for tonight, John?' asked Thomas.

'As ready as I'll ever be,' John whispered. Thomas looked at him nervously. 'No contact from the steward?'

John was deep in thought, then looked up. 'No. he said to stay away from the manor and keep to the plan.'

Thomas placed his hand on his shoulder. 'William and I will be right there with you. We will come with you to the alehouse and once the manor court and the rat baiting is over, we'll leave but hide off the road between here and home. Undercover of the dark, we'll follow you along, staying just out of hearing distance. If anything happens, we'll be there and so will the steward and his men.'

'I'll carry the torch, so you can keep me in sight,' replied John.

⁂

They allowed their eyes to adjust to the shadowy room to see several of the locals drinking ale and celebrating the end of the harvest. It was a festive mood, and all present were relaxed and social. Johnny Nutter, the baker from the manor was there and John Pigshells and Robert Deane.

'A season's work, while he sits up there in his hall sipping imported wine from distant regions and eating pheasant. Doesn't seem right, him taking our grain when we're the ones who grew it!'

'I hope he chokes on a bone,' said another, the ale relaxing his inhibitions. All who heard laughed, and then went quiet as the door slowly opened and the steward stepped in, his two deputies followed.

'What's this then? Have I walked into a bee's nest ready to be stung? Robert Deane what was that I heard about choking on a bone?'

Standing from the bench, Robert took his hat off. 'Nowt yer grace, right, I'll be on my way,' he walked toward the door. The steward stood in his path.

'Nowt yer grace, just telling the men how I almost choked on a chicken bone last night at supper.'

'Best you chew your food more carefully Robert Deane, I would hate for you to choke and leave Mrs Deane with a crop to tend and young 'uns to bring up lonely.'

'Aye yer grace, that would be sad indeed.' Nervously, Robert side stepped the steward and made his way outside, as did others fearing retribution from the chat that the steward had overheard.

The steward turned to see John. 'Ahh, Hargreaves, you're a bit early for the manor court.'

John stood, 'Aye yer grace, just popped in.'

'A little bird tells me you've been quite lucky at the games lately.'

John was nervous. 'Just potluck yer grace, no doubt won't happen again.'

Thomas looked at William and gestured toward the door, 'Right, we'll be off then, come on William let's get a move on.'

They left their jacks of ale half full, going quick smart through the door. Johnny Nutter followed them.

An old man sitting nearby walked up, poured the left-over ale from the three jacks into his, shrugged his shoulders, and guzzled the contents, a portion dripping from the corner of his mouth.

Outside, Johnny Nutter called out, 'THOMAS RUSHWORTH, Thomas. Can I 'ave a minute?'

William kept walking.

Thomas turned. 'Of course, you work at the manor with Agnes, right?'

'Yes, look, I need to talk to you about somethin'.'

'Go on then, what's troubling you?'

'Well, it's the cook at the manor…'

When Thomas arrived back at the cottage, he could see Margery outside collecting vegetables from the patch, bent over pulling the onions and black carrots and cutting a cabbage, then inspecting the underside of the leaves for pests. She ripped off the outer leaves which had been chewed by the looper and looked underneath, picking off the pupa which was firmly attached by a silky cocoon. Inspecting closely, she pulled a large green worm, arching its back, and kept it in her hand to be placed in William's wooden bowl on her cooking bench. She knew William liked to go fishing with them and it wasn't often that he came back empty- handed.

Thomas was deep in thought about what Johnny Nutter had told him outside the tavern.

He was disturbed by William at the door yelling out, 'Come on brother, we been waiting for ya', time's a wasting and John's here waiting for ya.'

'Yes alright.' Thomas quickened his pace and went through the door, the dogs followed him.

Thomas looked at John, who had a concerned look on his face. 'Alright John?'

'Yea,' replied John with a little apprehension.

'Right then, best we be off,' said William. Thomas walked over and gave his mother a kiss on the cheek. 'Terrar mother.'

'Terrar, be'ave yourselves,' she replied.

John, then Thomas followed by William, left through the door, the two big English mastiffs bounded after them

Margery could tell that there was something not quite right with Thomas when he left, but she couldn't figure out what. She went to the door. 'THOMAS, SEND THE DOGS BACK IT'S GETTING LATE.'

The sun started to go down, and there was a beautiful light over the moors. The dimming sun illuminated the dispersed cloud in a pattern of red and orange. Fingers of gold spread out from behind a chunk of cloud and threw its light into the expanse of the sky, then vanished, leaving a golden ribbon of gold on the horizon for a moment just before it went dark.

She went to collect the cow from the common green, walked him inside and guided the lamb in. Knowing it was that time, the chickens just followed, making their way to the corner of the cottage and up into the makeshift coop in the animal quarters. The rooster remained on the floor of the cottage, scratching at the straw for the fly maggots.

She lit the candles and walked to her cooking bench to cut the cabbage for the pottage the next morning and realised that her gutting knife was missing.

Why would one of the boys want with a gutting knife? Noooo must be around here somewhere, she thought to herself. Margery felt more uneasy and tried to shake off the disturbing thoughts. She remembered she probably took it out to the vegetable patch to cut the cabbage.

That was strange, she thought. She was never in the habit of leaving her sharpest knife behind but ventured out in the dark with a candle lighting her way. She got to the garden, then stooped near the cabbage patch, waving the candle left and right, thinking she may have dropped it.

She continued down the path, trying to remember where she may have left it. Suddenly, she heard a noise behind her. The dogs were silent.

Unlike them, with strange noises thereabouts, she thought. Then she heard it, a whine, then silence.

She walked towards the noise as the candle started to wane. Her eyes hadn't adjusted to the reduced light yet, so she stopped and allowed them to adjust. Continuing, she squinted, trying to make out what was in front of her. The dog was lying on its side on the ground; she walked over to look, placed her hand on its ribcage. It was breathing but laboured. It lifted its head to see her and whined again, putting its head back down awkwardly.

'What's up, boy? What have you done, poor thing?' She continued to reassure it, stroking the top of its head and neck, then she noticed some blood on the ground.

The dog continued to whine. She put her hand under its shoulder to see if she could help it up, but it wouldn't move. She pulled her hand out and it was covered in blood. Margery looked at her hand worriedly. 'What's this then?'

Gently, she felt its chest, using the dimmed candlelight she could see the wound. It continued to drain blood from the chest, just underneath the pit of its front leg. She walked quickly to the cottage and grabbed a blanket off the bed. Returning, she laid it out and pulled the dog onto it, but there was no sign of life. She felt its chest. It had stopped breathing. Saddened, she continued to pull the dog up to the cottage where it was lighter, but it was too late, it had lost too much blood and she could see the dark trail of dark red leading down to the vegetable garden. She went back with the candle to investigate, confused about why the dog was in there because she had closed the wicker gate.

With a new candle she started to investigate further, she noticed two more of the cabbages had been cut and another part of the garden had been uprooted.

Fearing the worst, she called out to the other dog, but there was no response. She went back to the cottage and wrapped the dog up in the blanket and pulled it in through the door.

Thomas and William will be so upset they loved that dog, she thought to herself as she wiped a tear from her eye.

She heard a noise behind as she straightened up and suddenly an arm grabbed her from behind. A knife, her knife, was held at her throat.

She tried to struggle free, but couldn't.

'Listen here you old cow, make a move or scream out and I'll cut ya' bleedin' throat. Now where's that bastard son of yours?'

'Let me be!' she yelled, trying to pull his arm away from her throat. He continued to jostle with her, then Stuart closed the door behind them.

'Keep goin' and you'll end up like the dog. All we want is that son of yours. If it wasn't fer him, we'd still 'ave our ears. Get us food, coin and some new clothes, while we wait for 'im. If ya cause us trouble, I'll slit ya' throat and we'll have him anyway.'

Margery could smell his onion breath and feel the spittle touching the side of her face, 'Go on then, take what ya' need but be off with ya' leave my Thomas, he's done nowt.'

He pushed her roughly toward the animal enclosure, where she lost her balance and fell to the floor. She turned and looked. He was a horrid little man with no teeth. His dirty red, straw-like hair bristled from below his red cap.

Stuart was already helping himself to the pottage, scooping some out with the ladle, blowing on it, and slurping it greedily.

'Have a look in that box for some clothes,' commanded the toothless one. 'Get us ale,' Archie looked at Margery with contempt.

Margery got herself up off the floor, straightened her kirtle and walked to her table, reaching underneath to get the clay jug. She took the linen cover off and filled two jacks, all the while hoping that Thomas and William would return soon. She put the jug on the table where the toothless one had seated himself. His companion was already trying on Thomas' Sunday best. The toothless one left the jack and reached for the jug, lifting it to his open mouth, pouring and guzzling until he choked, coughing then splattering most of the last gulp all over the table.

He wanted to keep her fearful. 'Give us bread and pottage old woman!' he coughed, still feeling some remnants of ale that had gone down wrong.

He coughed and then spat on the ground, snorted, trying to clear the ale, which was still lodged in his sinus, then spat again. Green phlegm came from his mouth and clung to the floor.

'Men folk are at the manor court, they won't be home for hours,' said Archie while lifting his filthy feet onto another stool.

Meanwhile, John and the boys were walking up Sun Street.

'Go home dog, what's wrong with you? GO,' Thomas yelled angrily. 'What's wrong with the stupid thing? She never ventures out this far. I spoilt her at the beck.'

'GO HOME,' William yelled, shooing the dog away.

The dog turned, sheepishly looking behind at his master, tail between his hind legs as he trotted away into the darkness toward home.

They arrived at the Kings Arms it was a lively night, and all were in lest they pay the fine. John saw the steward's men at a table playing cards. He got an ale and joined them as planned. Thomas and William stayed at the bar, they ordered an ale off the barkeep and William looked out for the serving wench. There she was. She smiled and winked at him as she walked back to the bar.

'Young William, will you be needing anything tonight?' She placed the empty jacks on the bar and picked up full ones.

William was just about to answer when Thomas interrupted, answering her question, 'No, he won't be needing anything tonight.'

'Such a shame, I'm in the mood for a sweet young cherry.' She turned and walked away with eight jacks between her hands.

William watched her walk away. 'She's a talented girl, that one. Her name is Lucy.' Thomas knew William had little coin, so assumed he was talking about the way she carried the jacks.

'Come on brother, you don't want to get mixed up with the likes of her. Half the men in the village and surrounds have been with her and besides, ya' have no coin.'

William looked over at Lucy. 'Well maybe I don't have to pay. Maybe she just has taken a liking to me.'

'Spoilt goods if ya' ask me,' claimed Thomas.

'Don't be rotten brother, she can't help it if it's the only way she can make a living!'

'Yer, well, let her find another to do the paying and the scrubbing afterwards.' As Thomas referred to her lack of cleanliness.

William started to get annoyed. 'Look at ya', all high and mighty now, just because you've got a wife.'

Thomas knew what his brother was like when he got his back up about something, trying to ease the tension. 'Brother, quieten yourself, I meant no harm, and if I did, I'm sorry, let's keep our minds on the job at hand.'

'What was that about a job at hand?' asked the barkeep as he noticed the heated discussion.

'Oh nothing, just arguing over who's going to shovel the shite in the mornin',' said Thomas, looking at William with disdain. He turned away, lifting the jack to his mouth to hide his annoyance. He looked over at John, who had already accumulated a tidy amount of coin in front of him.

William whispered to his brother, 'Do ya think they're here?'

'I don't know, but if they are, they'll notice John's winnings.'

William looked at the serving wench who was placing the jacks down on one of the tables. One of the drunks grabbed her and held her on his knee. She was shocked and tried to struggle free of him.

William was about to walk over but stopped when his brother put his hand out to stop him. 'Leave it be.'

The drunk had consumed his fair share. 'Come on sweetheart, how about a kiss?' She took her right hand and squeezed his testicles through the hose of the codpiece.

He went silent and grimaced, while all that saw and heard laughed with merriment. The serving wench, used to such treatment, had the situation well under control.

'Now Henry, you should know that nothin's for free.' She squeezed harder.

Worriedly, Henry's face went a bright red and he started to pant, 'Okay miss Lucy, please, let them go.'

The closer patrons, that could see what was going on, were in hysterics. 'Aye up Henry, you alright? Ya' startin' to look a bit red in the face.'

'Must have had a bit too much sun,' said another.

'Nah, he's hurting where the sun don't shine,' said another, prompting all to bellow with laughter, one choking on his last gulp of ale.

Lucy squeezed a bit harder. 'Now Henry, you know that this type of behaviour is frowned upon by the good old barkeep and what of the poor missis at home? What's she gonna say when she hears about your fraternisin' with another woman?'

Henry's face turned from a bright red to a pale white. 'Please, please let them go,' he whispered, placing his hands over hers.

The others turned away, having seen previous incidents by other unknowing patrons. Lucy played a hard game, and the locals knew not to mess with her. That was, unless it was upstairs.

She reduced the strength of her grip. 'Now Henry, quite happy to, but I want to hear you ask nicely. Say after me, "Ms Lucy, please forgive me for my misguided ways, I promise not to disrespect you in such a way again".'

Lucy increased her grip, Henry gasped again.

'Ms Lucy, please forgive me for my misguided ways, I promise not to disrespect you in such a way again.'

Lucy continued to hold on. 'Right, as I said before, nothin's for free, that'll be three shillings Henry.'

Henry reached into his purse. Lucy could hear the jingling of the coins. 'There, now let me go for Christ's sake.' Henry placed coins in her hand.

'Thank you.' She stood up and continued collecting the empty jacks as if nothing had happened.

Henry breathed a sigh of relief and re-adjusted his codpiece. 'More ale gentlemen?' Lucy walked toward the barkeep.

'Everything alright Lucy?'

'Yea 'course, the boys were just having' a bit o' fun, no harm done'.

William couldn't take his eyes off her, paying far more attention to her cleavage than was polite. She caught him looking and winked at him. Blushing, he took a swig of ale and looked away. She walked over to pick up the full jacks that the barkeep had put on the bar for her. Standing right next to William, she leant over and whispered. William put his head down to receive the whisper, also receiving a close up of her cleavage, which he relished. Thomas looked over and shook his head in disgust.

'Seein' as you're such a gentleman, I saw you about to walk over when he grabbed me, and I've already been paid tonight, how about I give thee a special rate?'

Stuttering, 'I-I can't tonight, I got b-business.'

'Well, when you get coin you come back.' She winked at him, turned, picked up the jacks and walked away. She could feel his eyes follow. Thomas shook his head.

Still watching Lucy, William spoke, 'Say nowt brother, you're not me father and if you were, I'm old enough to make me own decisions so say nowt!'

Thomas looked over at John, who had a smile on his face and continued to retrieve coins from the middle of the table. The steward's men played along, complaining about their poor luck. They did it loud enough for all to hear and see.

At that point, the door opened and the steward walked in, followed by the rat catcher with his rats. The steward had already given his men money to wager, so he went to the bar to get his pewter mug of ale. The rat catcher disappeared down the old wooden stairs and William and Thomas followed.

'Looks like the rat baitin's about to start so I'll give thee a chance to win back some of yer coin afterwards,' said John as he stood from the table.

'Right, you are then,' said Captain Smythe as he adjusted his eye patch.

'Yer, and make sure ya do,' said Joseph Moore as they stood and followed John down the old wooden stairs.

'Twenty-one,' whispered the captain. John stopped in the middle of the stairs and looked around with a quizzical look on his face.

Captain Smythe whispered again, 'Twenty-one!'

John turned and continued down the stairs into the old stone room. It was abuzz with all manner of chat, arguing, put downs and accusations about the health of the dog and the size of the rats who had already been poured into the pit. Billy was growling and barking, excited by the squeal of the rats and the motivations of his owner. One rat had already succumbed to the experience and lay motionless. Another retreated, running along the base of the wooden wall to the other side of the pit where he sat on his hind legs and started preening himself. The referee walked into the pit and removed the dead rat, picking it up by the tail and chucking it over to the corner of the room. The other rat, seizing his opportunity, followed the base of the pit and quickly escaped through the open partition. Billy saw the rat and took off in pursuit, only to be choked by the rope tied around his neck.

Thomas and William waited a few moments and then followed, looking for John as they ducked their head at the bottom of the stairs. They walked over to him. Thomas patted him on the back as he leant on the perimeter wall of the pit.

'Ya' alright John?'

'Yer, fine. Belly full a' ale and a purse full a' coin, couldn't be happier. Look, take this and have a wager.'

John discretely placed four shillings in Thomas' hand, then whispered, 'Twenty-one's the number,' as he walked away.

Thomas was confused. 'What? I can't hear him, did he say twenty-one?'

William shrugged his shoulders, still having thoughts of the cleavage of Lucy, the barmaid, who by now was probably busy two floors up.

Thomas leant closer to William, he whispered, 'Here, take this and have a wager on twenty-one.' Thomas placed two shillings in William's hand, turned and tried to conjure up a bet. 'Twenty-one I reckon, anybody for twenty-one? Odds three ta' one.'

'Yer, I'll take those odds. Bloody hell, the dog struggled last time, I'll give ya' your odds,' said the cook from the manor confidently.

Watching Thomas and the other men, William raised his hand and shouted out, 'Twenty-one, three ta one odds.'

'I'll give ya' yer odds lad,' said the cobbler standing behind him.

'Come on Billy let's show 'em what you can do', said the owner stepping forward. He took the rope off the dog and picked him up by the scruff of the neck, holding him in mid-air on the inside of the pit. The crowd roared. The spectators screamed their bets backwards and forward across the pit.

The dog, seeing the rats, was in a frenzy and tried to struggle free from his owner's grasp, but he couldn't break his grip. The owner looked at the marshal and waited for the signal. When the marshal nodded, he dropped the dog. The timekeeper turned the minute glass as soon as the dog's paws touched the floor. Excitedly, Billy growled and flew at the rats, his senses alert and keen, he was ready to do what he had been trained to do.

The dog bolted, he was in a frenzy, a grip, a toss and it was all over for the rat. They scattered as he approached, but he was too quick and knew their habits, running close to the wall as tight as they could.

The marshal called out the number of rats, 'One rat, two, three, four, five...' Some lay motionless, others bloodied with their entrails following behind them. 'Seventeen... eighteen... nineteen... twenty... twenty-one, TIME!'

The marshal lifted Billy by the scruff of the neck, out and back to his owner. Billy wasn't finished yet so tried to fight his way out of the referee's grip almost biting him on the hand.

Thomas and William both stood there, saying nothing, but shocked at the events that had just unfolded before them. They collected their coin and noticed John on the other side of the pit collecting a handful of shillings from the cook from the manor.

There was the usual name-calling and derogatory comments about the dog and the owner. One who had lost his coin for the fines entertained the idea of taking the dog for a walk over the moors. Another mentioned the beck and something about a heavy rock. Billy's owner picked him up and climbed the stairs quickly and disappeared through the crowd and out the door.

The barkeep had already positioned the tables for the jurors and the clerk, and the steward sat for the proceedings. The steward heard the call of the night watchmen from down the street.

The men that were downstairs returned, the room filled with all those that had business and more.

Sitting at the end of the table, the steward watched the clerk take money for fines and watched as he proceeded to make notes in his ledger.

William and Thomas paid their two shillings, then gave back the money John had given to them to wager but kept the winnings. John had shillings in his purse and took a handful out to pay the clerk so that all could see.

'Come on Thomas, William, I think there's ale to be drunk,' John walked over to an empty table and they followed.

William sat and looked at the shillings in his hand, mesmerised by their texture and weight. He held one to the candlelight and looked at the inscriptions. He could make out the face of King James and the English coat of arms on the reverse side.

Lucy came over to the table and noticed William toying with his shilling. 'Ayup gents, ale all round? You better spend that soon, William, before you wear the silver down to nothin',' knowing William would understand her meaning.

'Yes, ale all round and have one for yourself.' John flipped her a coin which she cleverly caught with her free hand.

'You're a generous man tonight, John Hargreaves. Win at the baitin' did we?'

'Yea and keep the ale comin',' said John, knowing she would make sure his win would get to enough ears to spark interest.

'Three ales comin' up,' she walked to the barkeep and put the shilling on the bar. 'Seems like those likely fellas have done well at the baitin',' whispered Lucy.

'Is that right?' the barkeep poured, filling three jacks and placing them on the bar for her to take back.

'There ya' go gents, let us know if ya' need anythin' else, anythin' at all,' she said, winking at William. John took a guzzle of ale greedily, some spilling from the corner of his mouth and dripping onto the table.

He looked for the steward's men but hadn't seen them since they were downstairs. He assumed they had gone to prepare, he relaxed and enjoyed the celebrations with Thomas and William. They had barely finished their last gulp when Lucy replaced them with new ones. William found it hard to keep up and found himself with a couple of full jacks collecting on his part of the table.

'Come on lad, keep up, not often we can celebrate in this style,' said John as he and Thomas downed another, then another after that.

Thomas had been thinking about what Johnny Nutter had told him about the cook at the manor. 'John, there's something serious I need to discuss with you.'

'Aye, and what's that?'

Thomas leaned in and whispered, 'Baker at the manor told me the cook, well he's been getting a little heavy handed with our Agnes. I've noticed the welts on the back of her legs.'

Hargreaves frowned. 'Has he now? We will have to pay a little visit to the manor but first things first.' He winked.

'Don't look now, he's sitting over there.'

Feeling bloated, William sculled the second jack and then another and then let out a loud.

'Buuuuurp.'

CHAPTER 19

IN THE SHADOW

By this time, Archie and his companion had changed their clothes and had their fill of pottage and bread.

Margery could tell they were starting to get a bit tipsy from the ale that she continually topped up.

She noticed the fire was dying down. 'I should get some more wood for the fire,' she said as she started walking toward the door.

Archie grabbed the knife from the table and quickly stood. 'Oh no ya bloody well don't. Do ya think we came down with the last rains? Stay where you are, I'll be gettin' the wood.'

Archie gave his companion the knife and walked toward the door. 'Watch her carefully and don't turn ya' back on her, no funny stuff you.' He pointed to Margery in a threatening tone.

※

The dog was trotting home, ears bouncing and drool splattering, her tongue flapping out the corner of her mouth. She passed over the freshly harvested wheat field, stopping to squat and urinate at the tree where they liked to sit in the shade on a hot summer's day. She could see the welcome light of the cottage but was confused she was not greeted by the other dog. He was probably dozing next to the fire. As she got closer, she could hear some unfamiliar voices and realised something was not right. She stopped, raised her snout sniffing for unfamiliarity. The English mastiff could hear a threatening tone coming from inside.

Nearing the cottage, she could smell another odor, more menacing than the sound. Snout down, she sniffed one way, then the other. In the dark she smelt it, the trail of blood, so she followed it quickly to the door. There was the pool of blood that had soaked into the dirt which she sniffed. The mastiff picked up on the scent of strangers, which alarmed her. She could see the door opening and the scent and figure of the man was unknown.

Inside the cottage, Archie lifted the latch, took one more look back at Margery, then took one step into the night. The huge beast barked, then growled and jumped up at him, almost as tall when standing on two paws. The mastiff pushed him back, and he fell to the floor with her paws resting on top of him. He put his arms up and the dog bit his arm.

Archie screamed, 'GET IT OFF GET IT OFF!' while trying to push its large muzzle from his face. His companion took one step closer with the knife, but seeing how ferocious the dog looked, thought better of it. He remembered how Archie had given him up at the manor court.

The beast shook her giant head to remove his hand, then latched onto his three fingers, biting down hard. The three fingers were partly severed and now began to dangle loosely.

He screamed again, still trying to push the dog off, but now made harder with one hand badly injured as the fingers bled profusely.

Margery said nothing and didn't move for fear of the other stranger with the knife. Suddenly, he dropped the knife, climbed on a stool and jumped out the open shutter into the night.

'Get him dog,' said Margery in a low, demanding tone.

'NO NOOO CALL HIM OFF!' screamed Archie.

She became even more ferocious at the command and latched on to his face, biting into the skin and severing his nose from his face, making it a bloodied mess. As he continued to scream, the dog latched onto the side of his throat, the teeth perforating his jugular, which started to pump and bloody the dog's snout. He grabbed the scruff of the neck, trying to pull it off with one hand, but the dog was too powerful, and he could feel himself getting weaker. Archie tried to loosen the dog's grip with his lame hand, but each time he moved the dog would latch onto his throat tighter. Eventually, the dog moved her teeth over his Adam's apple and bit down with force, crushing his larynx. The toothless one stopped struggling and went silent. A pool of blood started to spread on the earthen floor, staining the straw a crimson red. The dog released her grip but stood on his chest with her front paws; her tail erect, looking down at him, growling. She lowered her snout close to his face to look for signs of life, there were none. Then she looked at Margery who was standing on the other side of the table.

Margery looked down on the victim. She felt a queasiness looking at the bloodied face and the neck which continued to seep blood. She could see his nose hanging to the side of his face and the dark hole which it once covered. Margery walked outside to get some air and the dog wagged her tail and followed. Margery felt traumatised by what had just happened and started to sob. She patted the dog and scratched it behind the ears and hugged it for comfort. The English mastiff lifted her snout to test the breeze and could smell his scent. Quickly running inside, she took another sniff of the corpse now becoming cold on the floor and went to the corner of the room. The other mastiff was bundled up in a blanket with just his snout protruding from it. She sniffed and then whined, pacing up and down the length of his body, then licked his snout hoping that he would wake, but he didn't. She sniffed the dark bloodied patch on the blanket and whined again, then barked loudly trying to wake him.

Margery walked inside, kneeling beside the dog. 'I'm sorry girl.' She put her arm around her to comfort her, slowly scratching the scruff of her neck.

The dog barked again trying to wake him, but saddened, she lifted her snout up to the ceiling and howled soulfully then whined and laid down, her snout close to his. There she stayed.

⸙

Back at the Kings Arms, Thomas wanting to better his brother, sculled the remnants of the last jack and then let out an even louder, 'Buuuuurp.' They both laughed. 'Wait for it.' John took another swig and started to conjure up a belch. Looking down at the table, he breathed in a couple of times to accumulate air. 'Wait for it.' He then let go with a tremendous baritone noise. The sound lingered for what seemed like an eternity and even the men at the other tables paused their card game, turned and looked. Satisfied, John smiled. Thomas and William smiled with him, then they all broke into laughter.

'More ale,' yelled John, looking around for the serving wench. He noticed the candle holder hanging from the ceiling swinging and went to the bar himself. He was a little tipsy and walked unbalanced up to the barkeep.

'Threeee more barkeep,' he said, trying not to slur his words. He put another shilling down. 'And keep them coming.'

He took the jacks back to the table and placed one in front of William, then Thomas.

'John, we've had enough,' stated Thomas, looking dazed and shaking his head to wake himself up.

'Gew on, one more, we're celebrating,' claimed John disappointedly.

'John, we've had enough,' argued Thomas.

Thomas stood, sculled his drink then walked toward the door with William following close behind, albeit a little gingerly on his feet.

William looked behind just before leaving the room, scanning the room for Lucy. She was nowhere in sight. *Probably busy upstairs*, he thought to himself sadly.

John stood, sculled the rest of his drink then walked out the door behind them. He adjusted his eyes to the darkness and followed in their general direction. He could hear them in front of him, but their voices slowly started to fade as they quickened their pace to get ahead of him.

The barkeeper stood behind the bar, pouring the leftovers from the jacks left on the tables into a tankard to be mixed in with tomorrow's brew. Picking up an empty jack from the bar, he spat in it and continued to wipe and polish the inside, then placed it on the shelf behind him.

By now, most of the tables were empty except for one. The steward remained, counting his coin from the evening's takings by candlelight. 'Barkeep bring me an ale.'

The barkeeper, unaware of where Lucy had gone, brought the jug over and poured into the pewter mug.

The steward continued fondling his coin. In a low tone, almost growling, but not raising his head. 'Did you think I wouldn't find out about your thieving?'

The barkeep nervously took a step back. 'I swear to ya' yer grace, I've done nowt.' He looked down at the steward, reaching behind to clasp the small blade that was sheathed in the back of his hose.

The barkeep took another step backwards. 'I swear I've done nowt.'

The steward looked up at him menacingly. 'Lucy has told me everything. Unfortunately, she's come down with a bit of a sniffle, so she won't be here to help ya' close for the night.'

Lucy was upstairs and she looked down from above through a knotted hole in the floor. She had been escorted up to the room numerous times by the steward's manor staff. They would bounce up and down on the bed, swing the chandelier and make the floorboards creak. She was always careful to only flirt with those that she knew couldn't afford it, lest she raised suspicion.

The alehouse was one of the few places in the village where men spoke of their secrets and going backwards and forwards to the tables with full jacks and empty jacks, provided her with enough information about what was happening around the village. She kept the steward updated and he paid her.

The steward had a bad feeling about the barkeep from the very beginning. He knew he had been skimming coin for himself, but couldn't prove it until Lucy told him.

It had taken her months to figure out how he did it. She eventually noticed how he, with sleight of hand, dropped coin into his upturned sleeve. The rest was just a stage show, a stage show that she had become very good at. When she went upstairs, she would look down at the barkeep through the knotted hole in the floor.

Downstairs a flash here, a flirt there to keep the barkeep unaware of her ruse. Most of the time, when she flirted with one of the men, it was to hear what was being said at the next table.

Except that William Rushworth, well he was just cute, she thought, but she knew she couldn't mix business with pleasure. The steward kept his head down and continued to fondle his coins in the light of the candle. 'Now then, the way I see it, you have two choices, the first, is ta take your hand from the blade…'

The steward, who had his right hand on his knife concealed just under the inside of his thigh, stood at lightning speed, knocking both his table and the stool over. He held the tip of his knife in the soft underpart of the barkeep's chin, the pointy tip piercing the skin just enough to worry him.

The barkeep, terrified, dropped his blade and lifted his hands in the air. He took a step back to try to release the pressure of the steward's knife, but the steward took a step forward to compensate. He marched forward. The barkeep tripped slightly and recovered, keeping his hands in the air, raising his chin to the pointy end of the knife until his back was at the wall.

'Now then, as I was saying, you have two choices.'

The barkeep groaned, 'I done nowt please take your blade from me throat.'

'I am sure you are somehow involved with the footpads who have been working the village, am I right?' The steward turned the blade to his throat.

'Yes, yes, okay! But I only gave them information I swear!'

'WELL? WHO ARE THEY?'

'They'll kill me if I tell you…'

Nathan Midgley, the Haworth night watchman had been watching the events unfold, appeared from outside. The steward was thankful for his presence.

'Orl right yer grace?' he took out his truncheon and walked up to the barkeep and looked him closely in the eyes.

'Want me to give him a hidin'? I'll get it out of him.' The night watchman grabbed his arm and turned him around. He pushed his face against the cold, hard rock wall with his hand, then took his wrists and shackled them. Grabbing him by the back of the hair, he reached around and felt the barman's sleeve. Unrolling it, he felt the coin and allowed it to drop to the floor. The steward smiled and bent down to pick it up.

The night watchman put one hand between his legs, grabbing his testicles and lifted.

'OKAY, OKAY, I'll tell ya'…'

The steward, quite impressed by the night watchman's handling of the situation, let him take the lead.

'Nathan, I must go. You seem to have everything under control,' said the steward.

'He won't be going anywhere, 'cept the lock up,' said the night watchman as he grabbed the shackles and attached a chain to them.

'Come on old son, let's get ya' up to North Street and get you all tucked in. You'll like the diggings; there's a straw mattress on the' floor, one square meal a day. What more could ya' ask for? If ya' behave, might even give thee a blanket.'

The night watchman opened the door, then roughly pushed the barkeep out into the street. He swung his truncheon as if it wielded some special power. They crossed the square and walked up Changegate, turned left on North Street to the lockup. It was just a small stone box, no shutters and one door, but the walls were smooth and thick, and the wooden ceiling was high. The night watchman lived in a small cottage attached to the side with his wife.

He opened the door and pushed the barkeep in to the cold dark room, then locked the chain to a ring on the wall. The chain was just long enough for the barkeep to lie down on the straw mattress, but his wrist dangled higher than his outstretched body.

The night watchman walked over and kicked his prisoner in the stomach. The barkeep's wind was knocked out of him, and he tried hard to get it back.

'Right then, you have a good sleep, and we'll see ya' in the mornin' oh and by the way, don't try ta get out, my wife's a very light sleeper.'

The night watchman kicked him again then walked out the door, slamming it behind him and locked it with the large iron padlock.

CHAPTER 20

THE COLD SILENCE

Thomas and William quickened their pace. As soon as they got to the bottom of Main Street they cut into the fields and walked parallel to the road, then stopped and waited. It was a full moon, but the cloud covered most of it, giving the night an eerie, foreboding atmosphere. There was a slight breeze, so they didn't say much, ensuring their voices didn't carry. A short time later they heard John walking along the road; he was whistling, so they knew it was him. He walked past them, and could see his outline shaped by what little light the moon provided. He continued to walk, and they followed, staying about twenty paces parallel to him. As they got to Marsh Lane, he became partly obscured by brush, but they could still hear him whistling.

'Where are they?' whispered William.

John walked past more cottages. He turned left on Moorhouse Lane and started to walk across the field toward home.

Thomas looked over at the main road then back at William. 'The footpads, they must have been scared off by something!'

'What about the steward 'n' his men?' asked William.

Thomas was annoyed. 'Who knows, the steward was still in the alehouse when we left, didn't look like he was getting up from the table.'

Thomas and William relaxed a little as they kept on walking but decided to come up the back way to the cottage. They lost sight of

John but could still hear him whistling in the distance until it suddenly stopped.

When John opened the door to the cottage, they could see him in the glow from the fire.

By now, the two of them had sobered up and were entertaining the idea of walking straight home until they heard voices.

When John opened the door, what he saw scared the life out of him. Agnes and her mother were both gagged and bound, sitting on the floor, their backs against the far wall. As Agnes saw her father, she grunted through her gag and gestured for him to look behind, but it was too late. The masked man had already walked up behind him and placed his knife at his back. John took a step forward to escape the blade, but the man moved forward to keep it in contact. John stood there motionless, hands held high. He could see the fear in Agnes' eyes and Margaret was grunting.

Margaret quietened as another masked man lifted his sword to her chest. 'If ya know what's good fer ya', you'll shut it,' he grumbled.

'What do you want? Let them go!' John tried to make out the man's face, but it was covered, and the only light was the glow from the embers in the fire.

'You know what we want, hand it over and we'll be gone,' said the footpad as he continued to hold the knife at his back.

The footpad cut the leather straps holding John's purse to his thigh. The purse fell to the ground, spilling coin all over the floor.

The masked man looked down at the coin. 'We have been lucky this evening, enough silver to feed a family for a week.'

As the footpad was distracted by the coin, John turned, quickly reached up and dragged the dark cloth from his face. The footpad was so fixated on the coin he didn't see it coming and was slow to react, dropping his knife, and trying to pull his mask up to cover his face again. It was too late. The footpad back handed John, knocking him backwards. He picked up his knife and held it against John's throat, cutting underneath his chin.

Agnes' muffled scream made the other footpad nervous, so he put the tip of his sword against her chest.

'That was damn right daft. All yer had to do was stay quiet and give us the coin, now you've complicated things, ya fool!'

'The deputy!' John whispered.

John bent over and picked up the purse and handed it to the deputy.

The other deputy took off his mask.

'But why?' John muttered.

The deputy frowned. 'Why? There was a time when Catholics ruled the nation. Now look at us, scrimping and starving. Our lands stolen, our families tortured and jailed. I see the steward skim the takin's from his lordship every week without as much as a farthing thrown to us! We're not here ta beg for his scraps! One day there'll be a reckonin' and the true faith will be restored.'

By this time, Thomas and William were about thirty paces from the cottage. They could hear strange voices, men's voices.

'Something's not right William.' Thomas stopped and crouched in the long grass.

William followed his lead. 'What's wrong brother?' he whispered.

Breathing heavily from his exertions. 'Listen!'

A muffled scream broke the silence, and they could hear men talking in an urgent, demanding manner.

'Hear that? It's Agnes. Somethin's wrong, let's go,' Thomas said fearfully.

Thomas and William stood, but just as they were about to take their first step toward the cottage, both were grabbed from behind; two dark figures put their hand over their mouth and had a good choke hold around both their necks. They were quietly dragged down into the long grass.

The steward put his hand over Thomas' mouth. 'Shush, you fool, it is I,' he whispered.

William still startled, panicked, breathing heavily through his nose. The choke hold was debilitating. William heard the steward's voice and settled enough for the man with the eye patch to release his grip.

Captain Smythe raised his finger to his lips, urging William to be quiet before taking his hand off. They both rolled onto their stomach to take up positions beside the other men and peeked through the tips of the long grass.

'What are we goin' ta do?' whispered Thomas.

The steward whispered, 'We've been waiting here for the right time to act. Captain Smythe and his companion have been after these two for some time.'

Thomas looked over. He could see the outline of Joseph Moore and Captain Smythe, they were used to such business, their swords drawn.

'Now what are we to do?' asked the other deputy.

The other footpad dropped his knife from John's throat and turned him around. 'Make a move an' I'll run ya' through.'

He pushed his face to the stone wall, tied his wrists with rope, gagged him tightly and then pushed him face first on the bed.

'Well, we've only got one choice; kill them and continue on to the Welsh border!'

'Just go, let us be, and we won't reveal your identity,' called out John in a panicked tone.

He turned over and lifted himself from the bed, sitting on the edge.

'What about the patrols? They'll be on the hunt for us.'

'I'd rather take me chances with the patrols than hang around here any further. Hopefully, by now they've stopped looking. We have enough coin, we should go!'

Agnes and Margaret grunted, hearing some of what they were saying. John felt helpless. He assumed that Thomas and William had gone home, and the steward and his men were a no-show.

The deputy whispered, 'Well, the way I see it, we're damned if we do and damned if we don't. Either way, if we're caught, we'll swing.

I'd rather take my chances with the patrols than shit myself dangling from a rope.'

'I say, let's take them out into the moors. There's a shovel outside.'

❧

Outside, the steward and his men had crawled to within twenty paces of the cottage. They could see the front door, but still hidden by the darkness and the long summer grass. Thomas realised that things had gone quiet, and he was worried. 'We have to do something and do it quick!'

'Patience,' said Captain Smythe lying next to him, 'there's a time and a place.'

'What do ya think they're gonna do?' asked Thomas quietly.

Captain Smythe stared at the door.

They all ducked their heads lower as the door opened and the deputy appeared. Nervously, he looked across the dark moors for any sign that they weren't alone. Satisfied, he went back inside.

'Now we've got a problem, they've taken their masks off. Whoever's in there now knows their identity, which makes them far more dangerous,' whispered the steward.

'Aye,' said Captain Smythe, 'leave it much longer and we'll find them dead. We need a diversion steward.'

The steward turned to Thomas and whispered, 'You've been in there Thomas, explain the layout.'

Thomas thought for a moment. 'Animal shelter opens from outside at the back of the cottage. There's a chimney and fireplace… and a loft.'

The steward whispered to Thomas, 'Right, you go back around and come up to the front door as if nothing's wrong. Call out let them know you're coming.'

'Aye yer grace, come on William, let's make haste.' Thomas started crawling through the grass.

'No William, you wait here,' ordered the steward.

Thomas crawled backwards until it felt safe to stand, then covered by the darkness, walked around and started walking up to the front of the cottage.

Thomas called out, 'AYEUP JOHN ARE YOU IN THERE? It is I, Thomas, just wanted to come and get my winnings.'

The local dogs started barking, not used to the noise in the night, other dogs heard and continued the repertoire of territory claim.

The deputy, shocked by the intrusion, put his knife to John's throat, lifting him to the door and whispered, 'Tell him you're in bed and you'll see him tomorrow. No funny business.'

'THOMAS I'M HALF ASLEEP, I'll see thee tomorra.'

By this time, Captain Smythe had crept around the side of the cottage and was standing right next to the door. Thomas could see him signaling with his hands to keep him talking.

'Is Agnes home, John?'

The deputy pushed the point of his knife into John's back.

John grimaced and frowned, trying not to make a sound. He shrugged his shoulders, not knowing what to say.

The deputy leaned closer, 'Tell him she's still at the manor.'

'NO Thomas, she's still at the manor.'

Thomas knew he had to stall. He took a step closer to the door. 'Is everything alright John? You seem distracted.'

'I'M FINE JUST TIRED THAT'S ORL, NEED TO SLEEP!' John had the sound of panic in his voice.

'Do ya' mind if I come in and wait for Agnes?'

'Probably not a good idea Thomas, I think she might be staying at the manor tonight, so she can get an early start tomorrow mornin', but I'll tell her you called.'

Captain Smythe looked at Thomas and signaled for him to continue.

'Aww come on John, I'm parched and could use an ale before the walk home.'

The deputy, his face starting to show signs of anger, whispered, 'Tell him to come in.'

The other deputy, not expecting this turn of events, took his knife out of the sheath ready for a fight. He had a worried look on his face.

'Don't worry. We'll bundle him up like the other three and then we'll be off.'

'I'm going to cut you free, you open the door and let him in. If you try anything, I'll kill the lot of ya, starting with the sweet young thing, understand?'

John nodded, then turned to allow him to cut the straps.

'Remember what I said,' he whispered, moving behind the door within striking distance and keeping the blade poised.

They could both hear Thomas approach the door and when the deputy thought he was close enough, he lifted the latch and opened the door slightly to allow John to appear.

Captain Smythe took a step backwards and kicked the edge of the door with all his might. The deputy went flailing across the room but recovered quickly, keeping his balance, weapon poised. The other deputy joined him in a show of solidarity. The two were so concentrated on the door, they didn't notice both Joseph Moore and the steward slip in through the animal door behind them.

John's heart was pounding. Sensing what was happening, he walked backwards, climbed over the bed then to Agnes and his wife. He trembled while pulling their gags down and trying to undo the ropes on their wrists.

The steward allowed Joseph Moore to enter first and stayed at the door of the animal shelter.

Captain Smythe now entirely inside the cottage raised his sword. 'STAND DOWN MAN YOU ARE CORNERED AND OUT NUMBERED!' The deputy, so fixated on the man with the eye patch, didn't notice his partner engage another man behind him until he heard the clash of swords.

Too late now, he thought to himself. Fearful of the man with the eye patch standing in front of him, he also engaged his blade. He shifted his body weight onto his right foot and lunged, but Captain Smythe took a step sideways and easily parried the attack, a far worthier swordsman than the deputy had envisaged.

The captain yelled again, 'I SAID STAND DOWN! IN THE NAME OF THE KING!'

Thomas entered and looked around the door to see John trying to undo the ropes of Agnes. He slid along the wall, trying not to get too close to the close quarter fight that was taking place in front of him. Once out of harm, he ran along the opposite wall to Agnes and started to untie her ropes, but they were too tight.

'Quickly 'usband!'

Margaret had a panicked voice, 'Quickly John untie me.'

Joseph Moore had become a good swordsman, having been tutored by the captain in the King's Regiment. They used to practice every day, so he could easily hold his own against the other deputy.

Captain Smythe was quite a tall fellow, and with the eye patch looked menacing. Hoping to resolve things without bloodshed, he moved to the left and raised his sword to parry another thrust, but this time countered, forcing the deputy back further. The deputy, fearing the worst after experiencing the captain's swordplay, dropped his sword and raised his hands.

The captain raised his sword to his neck and kicked his sword away from him. 'Good decision,' he said in a confident tone.

The other deputy seeing this, followed his lead and stood back, also dropping his sword. Joseph picked it up slowly as he held his blade to the chest of his opponent.

At this point, William appeared in the loft with a pitchfork ready for battle, having climbed up the outside of the stone wall into the loft.

Joseph, still holding his sword, ordered the deputy to go over and face the wall by the door. 'Kneel and put your hands behind you, both of ya,' ordered Captain Smythe.

The two deputies knelt in the straw, putting their hands behind them, allowing Joseph Moore to tie them together.

The steward walked over to the deputies, who were still kneeling.

'Captain Smythe would you please escort these two back to Haworth and put them in the lock-up until we decide what to do with them. Oh, and be sure to search them.'

'Will do your grace.' He cut the purse from the deputy's belt and pulled out a handful of coin. Seeing what Captain Smythe pulled out of the purse, the steward stepped forward. 'Oh and I'll take that.' He took the purse from his hand. 'We'll sort out the pleasantries later, agreed?'

'Of course your grace.'

The Captain and Joseph tied ropes around their bindings, allowing them to walk out in front. They pulled the deputies up on their feet, swords still drawn. They pushed them through the door. Joseph lit a torch.

'Come on Joseph, let's get these two back to Haworth. It's been a long day,' Captain Smythe pushed the deputy forward roughly. They started walking toward Moorhouse Lane. Joseph followed, putting his sword in its sheath, one hand on the torch and one tight grip on the rope.

There was a chilly wind over the moors, and the clouds had cleared, allowing a bright full moon to light the way. Captain Smythe looked at the stars with his good eye; they sparkled like diamonds.

The deputy turned his head to look at Captain Smythe. 'How did you find us?'

'We've been hunting you for some time, Charles Ferrers and Robert Ambrose formally of Baddesley Clinton, Warwickshire. It was Fawkes who gave you away, told us you were escaping to Wales. Your co-conspirators are dead. You will spend the rest of your days in the Tower of London or worse, but that is not for us to decide.'

Captain Smythe and Joseph Moore were former soldiers and now bounty hunters, acting on behalf of King James, to find all Catholics connected to *The Gunpowder Plot*.

⁂

By this time, Agnes and Margaret had been freed. Agnes ran at Thomas, clenching him with all her might. Thomas put out his hands and held her. She held on and wouldn't let go. 'Thomas I was so scared,' she whispered.

'There, there wife, it's all over.' He squeezed her gently to provide some comfort. He looked at Mrs Hargreaves and John. Mrs Hargreaves looked at him and gave him an encouraging smile.

John Hargreaves walked past, touching him on the shoulder. 'Thomas, best you take Agnes home now. I have some business to take care of.'

⁂

Captain Smythe and the others slowly pulled the rope holding their captives taut as they went up the hill. They could finally see the tower of the chapel in the moonlight. Their captives were quiet, realising they had been bettered and now had to pay the price.

Arriving at the square, they passed the Kings Arms, the sign outside swinging in the breeze making a slow grinding noise on the rusty pole.

'Who goes there?' said the nightwatchman.

'Who asks, tis Captain Smythe and friend, returning with two Catholic traitors to be held in the lockup.'

'Right you are then, follow me.'

'We will return in the morning to collect them and return to London,' said Captain Smythe.

'Very well, they ain't going anywhere.' After locking them away, the nightwatchman continued his patrol.

'Good night ta ya watchman, let's hope the sun rises quickly for thee.' They sheathed their swords. The Captain and Joseph made their way to their lodgings at the manor. Pleased that they had rid the country of two more Catholic traitors.

⁂

Agnes let go of Thomas, then turned and looked to look at William still brandishing the pitchfork. 'William, you are so brave.'

Thomas rolled his eyes. 'Come on William, let's get home, come down and leave the pitchfork outside.'

John put his arm around Margaret, something he never did, but the traumatic events of the evening prompted him to do so. 'Come on wife, let's clean up and get to bed.'

'Come Thomas, there's work to be done in the mornin'. Goodnight mother, goodnight father. I'll see you tomorra' after the manor's work is done.' Agnes walked toward the door.

William appeared. 'Ya know I was ready to pounce, don't ya' Agnes? If those men hadn't got things sorted, I would have sprung into action to defend thee.'

Thomas rolled his eyes, but this time William saw it. 'You know I would have brother. I was ready and willin'.'

'Of course, ya' were William, you're the bravest.' Agnes gently touched him on the cheek and then walked through the door. Thomas followed, then looked back to see William holding his face, smiling and looking pleasantly content.

The three of them walked home and as they neared the cottage, noticed the brightness emanating from the cracks in the shutters.

'Mother's awake. Now we're in for it. Maybe we should send Agnes in first to calm her?' William suggested.

Thomas sniggered at William's fear.

'William, we'll just pretend that nothing happened, just went to pick up Agnes at the manor to bring her home. She doesn't need to know about all the other.'

Excitedly, William turned to Thomas. 'What? That we're heroes and thwarted the footpads? It'll be all over the village tomorrow, especially when people go into the village.'

'Look, William, the less ma hears about this the better.'

Agnes smiled, thinking how funny it was that two grown men were still terrified of their mother.

The dog, still laying at the side of her cold, still friend, heard the footsteps before Margery did and started growling and baring its teeth.

Still spooked by the events of the evening. Margery stood and walked to the back of the cottage. 'What is it girl? The other's come back? Get him.'

'Mother, it's us.' The dog whined when it heard Thomas' voice and ran to the door, pacing backwards and forwards and trying to get a look under. It barked, then whined again. Margery walked to the door, lifted the latch; the dog bolted in Thomas' direction.

'Thomas, William, where have ya' been? I've been worried sick, there's been a terrible tragedy, the dog, I'm so sorry.'

Thomas reached down and patted the dog. 'Where's the other?' he asked used to them both greeting him when he got home.

'That's what I been tryin' ta say', there's been a death! The two coney-catchers at the tavern that night, they returned lookin' fer ya'.'

Thomas immediately saw the body lying on the earthen floor covered with a linen blanket, blood stains evident.

'Mother, are ya alright?' Thomas walked over and put his arm around her.

She put her face in her hands and started to weep.

'Thomas, it was awful! The dog, they killed him.'

'Come now, sit by the fire,' Thomas guided her to the bench and supported her while she sat.

Agnes walked in, then froze, lifting her hands to her face in shock.

William followed, noticing the body and saw his brother consoling their mother. He paused, 'Ya alright mother?' He walked past Agnes up to the body lying in the middle of the floor.

The dog, who had been standing guard over it, growled.

William lifted the blanket to have a look, dropped it and immediately turned his head away. He calmly walked past Agnes, back outside; knelt on all fours in the long grass, knowing what was to come. He braced for it, repeatedly swallowing the extra saliva, then his stomach started pumping in and out and a mixture of this evening's ale and this morning's pottage made its way up, he heaved, it felt like he couldn't open his mouth wide enough. It came in a stream of burning liquid stinging the back of his throat. He coughed, groaned and his stomach concaved once more, ready for the next onslaught. He heaved again, trying to spit the distaste from his mouth. The dog, hearing the commotion outside, went out to investigate. She walked up and started licking William on the face as if it was a game.

He spat out the remnants from his mouth, then wiped his chin on his sleeve. William took a breath, spat again and knelt there, hoping no more would come.

Agnes had come to her senses and joined Margery on the stool. 'Ya' alright Mrs Rushworth?'

'Agnes, you stay here with mother, 'cause I need ta tend to things.'

Agnes put her arm around Mrs Rushworth while Thomas, hearing the noises, went outside to see to his brother. When he walked out, William was still on all fours.

The dog was sitting upright beside him.

Embarrassed, William stood. 'Thank ya' brother. Must have been a foul bowl of pottage I had this mornin'.'

The dog returned to lie beside her mate. She sniffed his face and whined, hoping for a reaction, but got none. She whined and put her chin on her paws beside him.

Thomas and William lifted the blanket, and they both turned away as the fellow's face was uncovered. It was a bloodied, mangled mess of a face, deep teeth marks, a darkened black hole where the nose used to be. His neck, an open, twisted mess of mangled skin, deep bite marks and a crushed Adam's apple, which sunk into the depths of his throat.

They lifted and spread out the blanket beside the unrecognisable corpse. Lifting him by head and foot, they placed him on top. Thomas turned the other half of the blanket, so he was fully covered.

The dog stood, eyeing what was going on. She didn't like others interfering and growled at the corpse.

'Quiet dog,' yelled Thomas.

The dog stood down, still interested but compliant and loyal. She continued to watch with interest.

They picked it up, Thomas by the shoulders and William by the feet. William walked backwards carrying the lifeless stiff over to the cart. They unceremoniously threw it in and pushed the cart down Marsh Lane. At the bottom of the hill, they stopped and pulled the cart westward across a fallow field, then over to a natural bog on the next property. William took the shovel and, in the darkness, dug a deep hole which kept filling up with water. They placed the corpse in the hole and pushed it underneath the black surface. As it submerged, small bubbles started to congregate.

Thomas held the shovel on the body, pushing it down, lest it reappear, while William shovelled the peat and mud back into the hole over the top of it, patting it down with the back of the shovel. Thomas stood on the disturbed ground. He looked at William in the moonlight and they both spat on the grave.

After they had dispensed with the corpse, Thomas and William walked back into the cottage. Margery and Agnes were still sitting on the bench, recounting the traumatic events of the day. Agnes had her arm around Margery to console her.

Thomas, saddened by seeing mother and Agnes so distraught, was about to say something until he watched the dog walk up and lay down beside a bundle at the back of the room.

He walked over and bent down, scratched the dog behind the ears, looking at the bundled, lifeless dog, its snout protruding from the linen sheet. He cringed at the bloodstain.

Thomas was saddened by its parting. 'He was a good dog.'

'Aye, he was,' said William, holding back, but feeling a sharp pain of sadness growing in the depths of his throat. William grabbed one end of the bundle, Thomas the other. As they were walking out, Thomas lit a torch and William grabbed the shovel. The other dog followed behind.

Thomas lit the way. Over to the tree in the field where the dogs liked to rest in the shade during the harvest.

William started digging a deep grave. 'No critter is going to interfere with you, my friend.'

Thomas put the torch in the snag of the tree and helped William gently lift the bundle and place it into the hole, filling it in, saying nothing, but both feeling the sharp pain growing in the depths of the throat that they couldn't swallow away.

Thomas started walking back to the cottage, torch in hand. William followed, then turned, trying to make his voice as uplifting as possible, 'Come on girl.'

The dog whined, turned away, crawled up onto the raised mound, circled once, laid down and put her chin on her paws. There she stayed.

William followed Thomas. The door was still open, and Thomas allowed his brother to enter first.

Margery stood, as did Agnes, who walked over and stoked the fire. She looked behind to see Thomas walk through the door, turn and close it behind him. He turned and their eyes met. They said nothing but were comforted by each other's presence.

By the time the cock crowed, Agnes had already started running toward the manor. When she got there, the other servant girls were preparing the lord's breakfast, Johnny Nutter was baking bread, but the cook was absent. She sighed with relief, then went to the pantry and got the ingredients she needed to start the mixing.

A few minutes later, the door opened and the cook hobbled in. He said nothing, then limped toward the whipping stick. Agnes frowned and looked down sadly, *he must have seen me arrive late,* she thought. All in the kitchen went quiet as they watched him slowly pick up the stick and turn to face Agnes. Still, he said nothing.

She was shocked. His face was a mess; he had a black eye, and his lip was cut and bleeding. He took a step toward Agnes then raised his knee and broke the whipping stick across it, chucking it in the fire. Agnes and the other servant girls gazed at each other curiously.

The cook limped to the table and started preparing breakfast.

Agnes poured the desired amount of spices into the bowl with the flour and the water and started mixing. She looked ahead and smiled.

Back in London, Charles Ferrers and Robert Ambrose were committed, tried and sentenced to death for treason. Sometime later, they were dragged behind a horse along the streets of London to Westminster Yard where they were hanged, drawn and quartered. Captain Smythe and Joseph Moore were in attendance.

Shawline Publishing Group Pty Ltd
www.shawlinepublishing.com.au

9 781922 444660